OCT 0 4 2022

MAYA
AND THE LORD OF SHADOWS

BY

RENA BARRON

CLARION BOOKS
An Imprint of HarperCollins*Publishers*

Clarion Books is an imprint of HarperCollins Publishers.

ISBN 978-0-35-810633-3

22 23 24 25 26   PC/LSCC   10 9 8 7 6 5 4 3 2 1

First Edition

To the dreamers and storytellers
who never stop believing.
This book is for you

. . . and for my little boy.

ONE

Is that all you got?

ZERAN KNOCKED ME on my butt for the third time in a row. I growled while he stood there grinning like he'd won already. He was enjoying beating me way too much. Not saying that I had an ego or anything, but if I did, it would seriously be (a) bruised, (b) smashed, (c) deflated, or (d) all of the above. Definitely *d* plus enough humiliation to last me the rest of the school year. It didn't help that most of the godlings at Jackson Middle were on the sidelines or the bleachers watching our match, along with several other matches happening at once. The gym was enchanted so that sparring partners and their magic stayed in their designated space.

After two close calls with the Lord of Shadows, the orisha council had decided that we should be ready when the veil between our world and the Dark finally failed. Now that Ogun, the orisha of iron and war, was teaching us how to defend ourselves, I didn't have to go to math tutoring anymore. Nor did I have to endure watching Gail Galanis doodle on her paper after solving an equation in record time while I struggled to remember the order of operations.

I glared at Zeran. "Lucky shot."

"Face it, Maya," he said, flashing his pearly white teeth. "I'm better than you."

I pushed myself up from the gym floor. "Keep telling yourself that."

I will admit this much: he *did* have more training. Before Zeran switched sides, he had been a part of the Lord of Shadows' army of darkbringers. He—the Lord of Shadows, *not Zeran*—had commanded that even kids prepare for an all-out war against the human world. Like me, Zeran didn't believe that darkbringers and humans should be fighting. But the Lord of Shadows wanted revenge ever since my father and the other orishas imprisoned him in the Dark. And he wasn't the kind of supreme evil overlord who changed his mind or backed down. *Ever.*

So what if Zeran had more training? I was good with my staff—better than good. I spent hours practicing with Papa in our backyard before Ogun gave up his disguise as Jackson Middle's crossing guard and started self-defense classes after school. I glanced longingly at the staff propped against the gym wall. The god symbols carved in the black wood pulsed faintly. *Have you lost your mind, Maya?* the staff seemed to say. *We're a team. You need me!*

Together we'd kicked more darkbringer butt than I could count. The staff was a conduit that helped me direct my magic. But Ogun said it gave me an unfair advantage over the other godlings, so he never let me spar with it. Staff or not, I wasn't going down without a fight.

Pivoting on my right foot, I lunged at Zeran and jutted out my elbow. I had intended to hook him in his side, but he was ready for my move. When he predictably stepped back to dodge my attack, I shoved my palm into his chest and concentrated hard on drawing out my magic. It was so much easier with the staff. I could snap my fingers, and BAM . . . it was there. This was like trying to pull a loose tooth that still refused to budge. Instead of the big bang I was hoping for, sparks of magic lit up my hand for a hot second, then quickly fizzled out.

"Ouch!" Eli cringed on the sideline, where he, Frankie, and Eleni stood watching our match. "Come on, Maya! You've got this!"

Winston and another group of kids on the bleachers burst into laughter, and I cringed in embarrassment. Tay whispered something that made Winston laugh even harder. Candace yawned like Zeran and I were boring her to tears. Despite everything that went down last summer and at the beginning of the school year, some of the godlings weren't taking the threat from the Lord of Shadows seriously.

Ogun stood underneath the basketball rim with a clipboard in his hands, wearing a blue-and-white tracksuit. General, his massive bloodhound, slept at his feet with one floppy ear draped over his eyes. Ogun scribbled something down. He was always taking notes. I wondered what he'd written about me today. *Maya Abeola continues to struggle to call her magic without her staff. How disappointing.*

A knot was growing in my stomach just thinking about it. I had to get my head right. My very reputation was at stake. Zeran and I had a bet to see who won the most matches whenever we were paired up. Best of three. I'd won the first round, but this second match was not going as planned.

"Is that all you got?" Zeran asked mockingly, as he went on the offensive.

When he came at me, I ducked and swept out my leg. This time I connected, and he hit the floor, landing hard on the mat. He grimaced as he pushed himself up again. "Who's lucky now?"

We circled each other, both looking for the upper hand. Before my eyes, blue bled across his brown skin until he was the color of cobalt. Small horns grew from his forehead and spiraled away from his face. A barbed tail shot out from his backside. Jet-black wings sprouted from between his shoulder blades through the slits in his sparring uniform. He'd dropped his human mask and transformed into his true self—the darkbringer. Several kids swooned, which only made me roll my eyes. He was such a show-off.

Only last summer, darkbringers had attacked our neighborhood. Now I was friends with one. So much had changed in only a few months. I went from not knowing about magic to being a guardian of the veil in training. I found out that the Lord of Shadows had killed Papa's first family over a thousand years ago, all except my half sister, Eleni. He'd put her in a deep sleep and used her godling power to tear the veil. This evil-overlord thing was serious business.

Zeran whipped out his tail, catching me off guard. It sliced through the air an inch from my face. "Hey, no fair!" I said, diving out of the way. "I can't use my staff, so why should you get to use your *um* . . . extra limb?"

"You'll have to deal with plenty of *extra limbs* when you fight the other darkbringers," he retorted, his voice annoyingly calm. "And they won't go easy on you."

I didn't know why he had to sound so sinister about it, like I didn't already know that. And news flash: I didn't expect or want him to go easy on me. I turned to Ogun, who glanced up from his clipboard. "I'll allow it as long as you're careful with your barbs, Zeran."

"Careful with his barbs," I murmured under my breath. The same barbs could cut through my uniform and rip the skin from my back. Okay then, but I wasn't about to give up. I swallowed hard. Now that Zeran was in his true form, he would be faster and more agile, but maybe I could use that against him.

Underneath the basketball rim, General's floppy ear fell from over his eyes and he let out a long howl. Ogun shook his head, looking particularly annoyed. "It seems that a godling at the high school has *accidentally* turned everyone, including himself, into guinea pigs. August, please officiate while I sort things out."

"Nice," someone remarked, followed by a bunch of snickering.

August, an eighth grader with a face that screamed *straight A student*, stepped forward when Ogun disappeared into thin air. "Carry on with your matches, godlings!"

When I hesitated, Winston blurted out, "Little Maya is a loser like I've been saying all along."

Frankie shoved up her glasses, which had slipped to the tip of her nose. "She's already lasted longer than you did against Zeran."

"Get your eyes checked, dork," Winston countered. "I went toe to toe with that freak."

"You will refrain from name-calling, Winston," August

said, clearly taking his job seriously, "or I will have to report you to Ogun."

While I was distracted by the side conversation, Zeran took flight and slammed into me. We both hit the floor this time and rolled. First, he pinned me to the ground, then I had him. Another roll and he was on top of me again, his knee pressed against my chest. "Do you yield?" he asked, quirking an eyebrow.

I wanted to scream in frustration, but I could hardly breathe. "No!"

Zeran threw up his arms. "Why do you have to be so stubborn all the time?"

"It's one of my best qualities," I answered, forcing a smile.

Ogun reappeared and walked over to where we were sprawled on the floor. From this vantage point, he was so tall that it was like looking up the length of a skyscraper. "The match goes to Zeran."

"But I haven't yielded!" I protested, keenly aware of the indignity of my situation. Here I was, flat on my back with a darkbringer's knee crushing my chest.

"In all these months of lessons, you have yet to learn how to accept defeat gracefully, Ms. Abeola." Ogun clucked his tongue. "You must know that you cannot win every fight. No one can."

It wasn't that I wanted to win every fight, but I couldn't

afford to lose. How could I help protect our world from the Lord of Shadows if it still took me so long to call my magic without my staff? It wasn't enough to be a guardian of the veil in training. If it weren't for my mistake, we wouldn't be in this predicament.

Zeran stood up and offered me a hand. I took it, and he pulled me to my feet. I wasn't mad at him—not really. I was angry that I still wasn't good enough. When the darkbringers came, they weren't going to take pity on me or anyone else. We all had to be ready.

"Are you okay?" Zeran asked once Ogun moved on to call the match between Jaylani Carmichael and Nate Townsend. "Sorry if I was a little rough on you."

I sighed. "I need to be better."

"You're too hard on yourself," Zeran said. "You don't think I got better overnight, do you?"

I pursed my lips, feeling my anger disappear. "Thought you said that you were born good."

"You do have a point." Zeran laughed, then he shifted on his heels awkwardly. "I have to leave training early. I'll catch up with you later."

I frowned at him, and a nagging uneasiness edged at the back of my mind. I hadn't forgotten that at the beginning of the school year, Tisha Thomas had a vision that Zeran would betray me. "What's going on?" I asked, trying my best not to sound nosy and failing.

"Are you my babysitter now?" Zeran rolled his eyes, although there was no bite to his words. He grinned. "I'll see you tomorrow."

I swallowed my doubt and smiled back. "I'll beat you next time."

He was free to leave whenever he wanted. It wasn't like training with Ogun was mandatory, especially not for a darkbringer who knew more than the rest of us combined. As he turned to go, his horns, wings, and tail vanished, and his blue skin changed back to brown. In his human form, he could have passed for Lil Nas X's younger brother. I watched as he walked out of the gym without looking back.

By the time I grabbed my staff from against the wall, the god symbols had stopped glowing. I could have sworn the staff shuddered beneath my grip. Eleni came over to where I was still sulking after my crushing defeat.

"How do you explain Zeran disappearing yet again?" I asked. "What if he really is a spy?"

Eleni shook her head as if I had just told her that cornflakes grew on trees. "He helped you save Papa's soul and rescue me from the Lord of Shadows. That sounds very un-spy-like."

"But Tisha Thomas said it, and her godling gift is foresight," I said, pitching my voice low so no one else could hear. "She can see into the future."

"Why would you listen to Tisha Thomas?" Eleni crossed

her arms. "She can't hold water."

I frowned. "What does holding water have to do with anything?"

"I mean that she tells everything she knows." Eleni glanced over her shoulder at Tisha, who was chatting with her friends.

Eleni wasn't wrong about that. Tisha was the gossip queen, but ever since she came into her godling power, she'd been different. It wasn't like before, in fourth grade, when I told her about one of my father's fantastical stories. She had called me a liar and by the end of the day, the whole fourth-grade class was cracking jokes at my expense.

"Usually, I would ignore her, but she knows things," I said. "She asked me about the Dark before the celestials told the other godlings the truth."

"Maybe it would be better if you asked Zeran outright, Maya," Eleni suggested. "See what he says."

"Of course." I crossed my arms. "He'll admit that he's a spy for the Lord of Shadows. A double agent. And he would have gotten away with it too if it wasn't for those *meddling kids*?"

Eleni tilted her head to the side. "Is that a reference to that old cartoon about a dog and his human companions?"

"Yeah," I said, smiling. Even though I was still getting to know her, it was nice to have a sister. She always listened when I was worried about something.

I bit my bottom lip. This was the third time this week that Zeran had excused himself from practice early. Something was up, and I couldn't keep waiting for the right moment to talk to him. Eleni was right. I had to be straight with Zeran. "I might as well get this over with now."

Eleni and I left the gym just as Ogun started the next round of matches. Both Frankie and Eli were in the second group to go. Frankie squared up against a godling twice her side. I didn't see who the kid was, but I knew they were going to lose. She was the first of my friends to show a gift for magic, and she excelled at it. Not to anyone's surprise. She was a genius, after all. Eli had already dropped into ghost mode and his opponent was throwing wild punches.

"Hey, Zeran!" I called after him.

He stopped and turned around stiffly. "What is it?"

"Well, I wanted to ask you something . . . something important."

I felt a tingling along my forearms, like static, only a hundred times worse. It snatched my breath away, and I forgot all about talking to Zeran. Dread climbed up my throat, and Eleni and I exchanged a knowing glance. Her face had gone blank.

"Another tear," we both said at the same time.

Eleni grimaced. "It feels far."

"Like on the West Coast far?" I guessed.

"Yeah," she answered.

Zeran glanced at his watch. "The other thing I have to do can wait. I'll come with you."

There was no time to get Frankie and Eli. The recent tears in the veil were big enough to let through hundreds of darkbringers at once. Papa had already been gone for hours with Eshu, fixing up tears across the world, so it was up to Eleni and me to close this one. I might have lost my match against Zeran, but this I could do.

Time to get to work.

TWO

HELLO, MY LITTLE NIBLING

OF ALL THE rotten places to find a tear in the veil, this had to be the worst. *Literally.* After Eleni insisted on opening the gateway, we ended up falling above a garbage dump. I plunged toward a pile of decomposing trash that smelled a hundred times worse than my old sweaty gym shoes. The symbols glowed on my staff again, shifting their positions quickly. The lion with raised paws was suddenly leaping across the sun, and the leaves on the tree pulsed like Morse code.

Mayday. Mayday. Death by trash pile at six o'clock.

"Wings!" I shouted at the staff as the massive pile of garbage soup grew closer. Was it my imagination, or was the trash sinking in the middle like it had opened its mouth to eat me? "Um? Hello, staff!"

I could feel the symbols shudder underneath my palms, but instead of wings, the staff let out a low hum. Was it still mad that I hadn't been able to use it in the sparring match against Zeran at school?

I was about two feet from the pile when a blur of black wings and blue skin fluttered across my vision. Zeran grabbed my arm to keep me from hitting the trash pile. The staff finally sprouted wings at that exact moment and smacked him in his face. Its purple feathers flew everywhere. Tell me that wasn't on purpose. I dare you.

Zeran winced and let go, and the staff melted into a harness that latched on to my back with ease. He spat out feathers and glared at me. "Do you have to be so rude?"

"I didn't do that!" I said, defending myself. "The staff has a mind of its own."

"No self-respecting thirteen-year-old I know would let their magic be so unrefined." Zeran landed on a strip of ground free of garbage. "I mastered my magic when I was like eight."

The *like eight* part was his way of rubbing it in my face that he was much better at magic than me, as if kicking my butt on the mat weren't enough.

Eleni hovered over our heads, looking angelic with the way flecks of gold shined in her curly amber 'fro. Six months ago, I thought the aziza—the forest fairies known for their beauty and for being notoriously wary of outsiders—were only something from Papa's stories. That was before I found out that I had one for a sister.

"It's very inconvenient that you don't have real wings, Maya," she said in her singsong voice, her own iridescent wings shimmering blue, purple, and pink under the fading afternoon sun. "We can't always expect to land on our feet, you know."

I resisted the urge to remind her that I was patching up tears in the veil with Papa long before Zeran helped Frankie, Eli, and me rescue *her*. We'd gone everywhere: oceans, swamps, underground caves, the desert, you name it. All without wings.

"Oh, I'm sorry I wasn't born with wings," I said, annoyed. "I'm neither an aziza nor a darkbringer. Just a plain half human and half celestial here."

"I'm sure Papa could give you some permanent wings if you ask," Eleni said excitedly. "They could match mine, and the other godlings would be so jealous."

"I'm good with my *fake* wings," I said. The harness fluttered excitedly against my back, and the wings lurched forward to pat me on top of my head. I guess we were on good terms again. "Stop messing around. We've got a tear to close." I landed on the ground, and the harness turned back into a staff.

Zeran wrinkled his nose. "I don't like this."

"Well, we are in the middle of a garbage dump, but you're right . . . something's off," I said as we picked our way through the towering piles of what had to be the worst-smelling trash on earth. I had to breathe through my mouth not to gag, but that barely helped.

"What I don't get is how the Lord of Shadows is still able to tear the veil if he's not using my power to do it." Eleni hovered next to me, her wings propelling her forward. "There's no way you could've damaged the veil that much."

"Me?" I huffed. "As I recall, the Lord of Shadows used that power-stealing coffin—"

"You mean the amplifier," Zeran interrupted.

"He used the amplifier to steal both of our powers to burn the veil," I finished.

"True, but had you never come to the Dark, he wouldn't have been able to do so much damage," Eleni said calmly in her sweet voice.

"If I hadn't come, you'd be asleep for another thousand years inside of that coffin . . ."

"*Amplifier*," Zeran mumbled, and I glared at him.

Eleni broke into a broad smile that looked like bottled-up sunshine. "I'm so glad you came."

"This is all touching, but we've got a tear to find, and the Johnston twins are expecting me home by six," Zeran said. "Miss Ida is making a strawberry cheesecake for dessert, and I don't plan on missing it."

"Oh, was that why you were in such a hurry to leave sparring practice early?" I asked innocently. "Strawberry cheesecake, *hmm?*"

Zeran swiped his tail back and forth like he was swatting flies. "Are you always this nosy, or do you especially care about what *I* do in my spare time?" He wriggled his eyebrows at me, and I stumbled over a soggy paper bag.

I scoffed and waved my hand dismissively. "Don't flatter yourself."

As we waded around piles of smelly trash, I still couldn't believe that Zeran was really here. Never in a million years did I think a darkbringer would turn against the Lord of Shadows, and he did it while defying his father, Commander Rovey. He had tried to rescue his little brother, Billu, who'd been taken to train with the most powerful darkbringers. Zeran had wanted to save him from that life, and so far, he'd failed. I watched as he disappeared behind one of the mounds of trash. I still had to talk to him about Tisha Thomas's vision, but that would have to wait.

"I miss picking strawberries with my sister, Kimala." Eleni's wings fluttered nervously against her back. She always did that when she was thinking about her family. She swiped at her eyes. "I miss playing hide-and-seek in the forest with Genu. I miss my mom . . . I miss my old life."

I squeezed her hand, and she shuddered. "I know it's not the same, but I'm glad that we're a family now."

"I'm glad, too," Eleni said, trying to sound brave.

As we walked around another pile of garbage, we heard a crash from up ahead. Eleni took flight, and I ran with my staff ready. I came to a stop when I saw Zeran sprawled on the ground with a foot planted on his chest. He was clawing at the leg of the person holding him down, but they only dug their boot further into his ribs.

My heart sped up as I raised my gaze and came eye to eye with one of my worst nightmares. Captain Nulan stood with her hands on her hips. It was hard not to see the resemblance between her and Eleni. They had the same golden-brown skin, curly hair, dimples, and iridescent wings. The Lord of Shadows couldn't do most of his dirty work without people like her, people who carried out his orders. One of his most deadly cronies had come through the tear—one who had almost gotten the best of my friends and me multiple times.

"It feels good to be back on this side of the veil," Captain Nulan said in a lazy drawl that sent ice down my spine. Then she turned her attention to Eleni and smiled. "Hello, my little nibling. Did you enjoy your nap?"

Before I could react, Eleni let out a soul-crushing scream and flew straight at her auntie. The same auntie who had betrayed her and her entire family. This was going to be epically bad.

THREE

THE WORST AUNTIE EVER

Captain Nulan dropped into a crouch and spun her back to Eleni. Her wings turned from iridescent to metal the moment before Eleni slammed into her. The impact sent Eleni flying backward, where she landed in a pile of shredded paper and gray sludge. Eleni shrieked as she sank deeper into the muck, and a rank smell that made my belly flip-flop filled the air.

Zeran tried to get up from the ground, but Nulan jammed her boot back into his ribs. "Be still, little traitor," she hissed at him. "You best be thankful that your father begged our lord to spare your life. Don't ever say he's not merciful."

"He can keep his so-called *mercy*." Zeran slung the word back at her. "I don't want it."

Eleni swiped hard at the tears streaking down her cheeks and accidentally spread bits of wet newspaper over her face. "I trusted you. Mama trusted you . . . You . . ." she stuttered. "You knew what the Lord of Shadows would do."

"I warned my sister about the celestials, but she wouldn't listen." Captain Nulan squared her shoulders, and her wings turned back to iridescent feathers. "She was doomed the moment she laid eyes on Elegguá. He was marked for death even then."

Eleni climbed to her feet. She was shaking from head to toe. "I won't let you get away with it."

Nulan had to be the worst auntie ever and generally an awful person. If she was in the human world, she was up to no good. I stepped beside my sister, my hand tightening on the staff. We would stop her *together*.

Nulan blinked. She had a bemused look, like she wasn't taking either of us seriously, which got on my last nerve. I wouldn't let her hurt my family and friends again. She'd already done so much damage. As I eased closer to her, two slender knives appeared in her hands. Magic tingled down my arms and vibrated in the staff. I wasn't going to back down.

"Don't do anything you're going to regret, little spawn." Nulan positioned her knives to strike. "Our lord still needs the both of you alive."

"He's already stolen our powers," I spat, my anger

flaring. I couldn't forget the moment I touched the amplifier and fell into Eleni's dream. While there, the Lord of Shadows used our combined magic to set the veil on fire. "What does he want now—*our lunch money?*"

"Wouldn't you like to know?" Nulan said as she flapped her wings and took flight. Finally free, Zeran curled on his side and coughed. "As much as I'd love to rip off your little fingers one by one, I've got business to take care of in the human world."

Magic shot out of my staff in bright sparks that flew toward Nulan. It curled into a rope, trying to latch on to her, but she surrounded herself in a cloud of fairy dust. The rope went limp and landed on a trash pile.

"Is that the best you can do?" Nulan laughed. "You've lost your touch."

"But I haven't," Zeran said as he rose into the sky. His eyes began to glow, and black clouds swelled over his head. Come to think of it, I'd never seen him use his powers beyond shapeshifting, so I didn't know what to expect. His father, Commander Rovey, could absorb other people's magic and turn it against them. Zeran raised his arms, and all around us, trash flew together. He smiled as random garbage reshaped itself so limbs jutted out in every direction.

"Nice trash spider," I called up to him.

Captain Nulan's knives disappeared, and she lifted her palm to her lips and blew. Silver dust spread across the trash spider and froze it in place along with Zeran. He glared at her, and she laughed even harder. No one could ever say that Nulan wasn't overconfident. She thought she was invincible, but she hadn't noticed that my rope was easing up behind her.

"Stop this, Auntie Tyana," Eleni said, closing in on Nulan. Real Talk: My sister smelled bad, like ten times worse than sweaty socks. She was covered in gray slime. Not her best look by a long shot. Although Eleni was focused on Nulan, I could feel the space shifting around us. It was subtle, like a sudden brush of cold air. *Is she opening a gateway?* "You must be punished for your crimes."

Nulan snapped her fingers, which turned my rope into ashes. "Not today, little nibling."

So much for her not knowing about it. Okay, time for plan B. Before I could think of something, several dozen arms raised out of the ground beneath where Nulan was hovering. They grew impossibly long and fast, like weeds shooting up in a flower bed. They latched on to her feet and legs. Nulan startled and struggled to free herself. "Argh!" she screamed. "Let go of me, you dreadful creatures."

Something flew across my line of vision and smacked Nulan across her forehead.

"Goal!" Eli said, suddenly appearing atop a pile of trash.

Frankie crouched beside him and shot a ball of electricity at Nulan. "Remember me?"

"I really hate children," Nulan groaned before the electricity turned into a net and knocked her out cold.

When Nulan hit the ground, ghosts, young and old, appeared, surrounding her—*Eli's army.* Unlike when we were in the Dark and he'd hijacked the darkbringer ghosts from the bog to help us break into the Crystal Palace, these were human ghosts. Zeran unfroze, and his trash spider disintegrated as he landed next to me.

***

"How did you get here?" I asked, happy to see my friends. It was almost like old times, except we now had Eleni and Zeran in our squad.

"You sent the gateway for us, didn't you?" Eli raced down the pile of trash, half slipping as a mini-avalanche slid under his feet.

"Imagine our surprise when the gateway suddenly opened as we were leaving training," Frankie said. "We were wondering what happened to you three."

"That was me," Eleni said with a shrug. "I thought we could use your help."

I turned to Eleni, awestruck. So she *was* opening a gateway, and she'd done it covertly. I had no idea that was even possible. Here I was still struggling with opening my gateways faster, and she'd already leveled up. I swallowed my jealousy as Frankie climbed down the mound of trash.

"Nulan said that she had business in the human world,"

I said. "We need to find out what."

"You're missing the bigger problem," Eleni said. "Auntie Tyana wouldn't come to the human world alone. Some of the darkbringers must've come with her and set off before we arrived."

Eli snickered with his hand over his mouth. "She's going to be so mad that the OGs outsmarted her again."

Zeran tilted his head to the side. "OGs?"

"Original godlings," Eli said. Then as if he'd forgotten that Zeran was a darkbringer, he added, "OGDs, in this case, but it doesn't sound as good."

"Did we outsmart Nulan?" Frankie said, adjusting her glasses. "Maya's right. We need to know what she was really up to. If people with as much magic as Captain Nulan can cross the veil now, that means . . ."

My throat felt papery. "It won't be long before the Lord of Shadows can cross himself."

"After I close the tear in the veil, we better get Auntie Tyana back to the orisha council," Eleni said. She lifted off and flew over a mound of garbage, where we could see the edge of the tear. It was like a cut across the sky.

Eli smacked his forehead. "Never a moment to celebrate before the next bad news hits."

"We got Captain Nulan," Frankie said. "I count that as a win."

"I better open a gateway in the community center," I

said. "I don't think the celestials will be happy if I open one in the gods' realm."

"Wait—you can't just open a gateway in the community center," Eli protested. "There are humans there. You're going to get us grounded for, like, eternity."

"Where do you suggest, Eli?" Eleni said, already done fixing the tear.

Even though she was covered in garbage juice and wet newspaper, Eli blushed. "In the basement. No one goes down there."

"Got it!" I said.

I drew my staff across the air, and sparks ignited in front of me, but Eleni was opening a gateway at the same time. Something weird happened. The two gateways snapped together like magnets, but instead of creating a super gateway, our bridges of god symbols intersected. At the point of impact, a burst of symbols—animals, planets, plants, geometrical shapes—arranged themselves in the form of a giant glowing egg.

"Oh." Eleni startled.

"What's that?" I asked.

She frowned. "I don't know."

"It looks like a kind of pocket in space," Frankie commented.

I lost my concentration, and the egg disappeared along with my gateway. "Weird."

Eleni's gateway turned back to normal. She shrugged as she started down the bridge of god symbols. Eli's ghosts marched behind her, carrying Captain Nulan. "Your gateways are always so nice," he said, kissing up to her.

I rolled my eyes. I was convinced that Eli had a crush on Eleni, though it felt like I was the only one who noticed.

I brought up the rear as we walked into the arch of dancing god symbols. My gateways were mostly chaotic, with symbols spinning wildly, the sound of roaring wind, and um . . . sometimes they lacked floors. In my defense, I'd opened most of them in a hurry. Eli was right. Eleni's gateways were works of art, ordered, calm, bright, warm, like sipping hot cocoa on a winter day.

This one was of an enchanted forest where the trees and grass were made of glowing god symbols. There were even chirping birds that reminded me of the winged star horses Papa had made to take Eli, Frankie, and me to Azur, the city in the clouds. Eleni had his touch. They were artists while I was still at the amateur level.

"Maya, I think you're right about Nulan," Zeran said, interrupting my thoughts. "We didn't see her by accident. She's too smart for that."

"Why do you think she's here?" I asked point-blank. Zeran was in the darkbringer army. He should have insight into their plans. I couldn't help but wonder how he'd let Nulan get the best of him so quickly, especially after he'd kicked my butt in training not an hour before.

"No clue," Zeran said hesitantly. He glanced away as if maybe he knew something but he didn't want to tell me. "My guess would be to stir up trouble."

"It's more than that," I argued, my nerves on edge. As much as I hated to admit it, if there was one thing we'd seen from the Lord of Shadows and his cronies, it was that they were smart and devious, not to mention calculating. "The Lord of Shadows has been planning his escape for too long to make rookie mistakes. We have to assume that there's more happening than meets the eye."

"Maybe Auntie Tyana is here to recruit the other magical creatures," Eleni suggested. "The ones who don't want to stay hidden."

"What do you mean, hidden?" Zeran asked, frowning. "Why should they hide?"

"It's not like in the Dark," Eleni explained. "The celestials forbid the magical creatures from interacting with the rest of the human world. It's too dangerous. Most of them were not happy about that. If I recall, some were sympathetic to the Lord of Shadows."

I almost asked who could be sympathetic to someone as awful as him, but Tyana Nulan was, and so were a lot of darkbringers. I thought about the elokos who had an appetite for human flesh and the werehyenas that had attacked Frankie and me last summer.

There were other magical creatures—the adze, vampiric fireflies, who preferred the blood of children. Chupacabra, haints, nyuvwira, goblins, and dozens of others. Most humans thought that these magical beings were myth and legend, but they very much were real. And some of them had very nasty reputations. They got a kick out of terrorizing people. I shuddered at the idea of Captain Nulan recruiting them to fight for the Lord of Shadows. "We have a sleeper army on this side of the veil who are sick of the celestials' rules," I mumbled under my breath. "That's bad business."

No one said anything as we crossed the gateway. What was there to say? We'd stopped Captain Nulan and foiled her plan, but I couldn't shake the nagging thought that the Lord of Shadows was already leagues ahead of us and we were busy playing catch-up. He was the cat, and he'd already set his deadly mousetrap.

FOUR

The first celestial

WHEN WE STEPPED out of the gateway into the community center basement, the fluorescent lights crackled to life over our heads, revealing dust-covered boxes and old equipment. A pinball machine sat in a row with several treadmills, half-deflated lifesavers, and a stack of CPR mannequins.

Frankie sneezed, and I wrinkled my nose at the moldy smell lingering on the cold draft. At least it was much better than the garbage dump. Eli's teeth chattered, but his ghosts were oblivious to the chilly basement. They held an unconscious Captain Nulan in their arms.

Eleni pulled Zeran aside as her fairy dust spread around them, alighting on their skin and clothes. They both glowed softly until her magic faded and, thankfully, with it, the muck and smell from rolling around in garbage soup.

Captain Nulan twitched in her sleep, and we all went still. None of us wanted to deal with the aftermath of her waking up. I wasn't convinced that Eli's ghosts and Frankie's net would hold her for long. "Let's get her up to the gods' realm on the double," I whispered.

"Time to go ghost mode," Eli said as he disappeared with his ghosts and Nulan.

Zeran changed back into his human disguise. "Can you handle Captain Nulan without me?"

I was about to protest him running off again, but Eli's disembodied voice spoke first. "Don't worry, bro, we've got this!"

Zeran jogged up the basement stairs. "Sweet—I have to run. See you all tomorrow."

I rolled my eyes. It was unlikely that he was *that* eager to get back to the Johnstons' house for strawberry cheesecake. We had Captain Nulan—*the* Captain Nulan, head crony to the Lord of Shadows. This was big, really big. The kind of big that earned a kid bragging rights for life, so excuse me if I thought strawberry cheesecake could wait.

"What were you doing down there?" someone demanded at the top of the stairs. It was Carla, the godling receptionist. She stood blocking Zeran's path. She was a little taller than him, with red glasses and a curly 'fro. "You better not be getting into trouble."

"Oh, the usual," Zeran answered. "Saving the world."

"In the basement?" Carla grumbled.

"It's a long story." Zeran ducked past her.

Carla shook her head when she saw Eleni, Frankie, and me come up the stairs. "I'm assuming the ghost boy is with you."

"We need to see the orisha council," I said.

Carla grimaced. "They're busy."

"I'm sure they can make time for this," Eli said as his ghosts flickered into physical form on the stairs, just long enough for Carla to see them and our prisoner.

Carla startled and stumbled back, her eyes glowing. She pointed one shaking finger. "That's Ty—Tyana Nulan. How did you . . ." She sighed. "You know what, never mind. I don't want to know."

Carla stepped aside as we climbed the steps. Eli and his ghosts went into stealth mode again. Eleni's wings fluttered against her back. Oshun, the orisha of beauty, had glimmered her so that only other godlings and celestials could see her true form, so we weren't worried about the humans who might be at the community center.

Most people in our neighborhood didn't know about godlings and the orishas. They didn't know about the Lord of Shadows, the darkbringers, or the veil between worlds. They didn't even know that there were other worlds, like many of them. I still hadn't decided if they were lucky or not. They got to live their lives without worrying about a scary man made of shadows with a bone to pick—a man who had no problem with wiping humans off the face of the planet. The celestials had forbidden us from revealing the truth. Only our human families knew—people like Mama, Frankie's moms, and parents of other godlings.

Carla opened a closet and turned on a light. "You can visit the gods' realm through here."

No one questioned her. Closets were handy places to hide secret passageways. That was how I first found a way into the Dark to save Papa when the Lord of Shadows had kidnapped him. As soon as we crowded inside the room next to the cleaning supplies, we started to ascend. It was like being on a high-speed elevator.

"Ugh, dirty mop water just splashed on my kicks," Eli said, grimacing at his shoes.

The previous times we had visited the orisha council, we'd gone through the metal detector next to Carla's desk, and we'd been pitched forward, not up. But before long, we were standing in front of the familiar two-story, golden doors that marked the gods' realm's entrance.

Frankie and I pushed open the doors into the starry nightscape. I inhaled a sharp breath and marched inside with my friends. My heart pounded with nervous energy. This wasn't the first time we'd shown up uninvited. I was beginning to see a pattern.

Lightning bugs nestled in the ceiling, and a cloud of darkness swelled beneath our feet. Four pillars marked the edges of the room, with nothing but endless stars beyond them. It was hard to explain the vastness of this place or the overwhelming feeling that I was standing in the middle of something so much bigger than I could ever wrap my mind around.

"Where's everyone?" Eleni asked.

"Carla said they were busy," I mumbled. "I guess she was right."

The gods' realm was empty except for the larger-than-life thrones that sat with their backs to the stars. "Nana!" Eli called with his hands cupped around his mouth. "We come bearing a gift!"

Frankie snickered and pushed up her sliding glasses. "That's an understatement."

Suddenly a pulsing light floated in from among the stars and melted into the shape of a woman. It was Oshun, the orisha of beauty. She strolled across the room in a gold chiffon dress with a long train behind her. She didn't even glance our way as she moved toward her throne. The other orishas appeared one by one.

Shangó, the thunder god, wore double axes across his chest. Ogun, the war god, strolled in next with his hammer. General, who had six eyes and a row of sharp teeth in his celestial form, trotted beside him. It was always weird to see Ogun like this when he wore a tracksuit during our defense training. Eshu, the god of balance, always reminded me of Papa a little. He had a bushy white beard and a harmonica on a string around his neck. Then there was Eli's grandmother, Nana, decked out in shades of purple with her gray braids pulled back into a bun.

Nana propped her hands on her hips, ready to give us a proper scolding until she saw who Eli's ghosts were carrying. "Do I want to know how she got here?"

"She crossed the veil, and we caught her," Eli said to his grandmother, thrusting out his chest. "Aren't we the most awesome godlings there ever were?"

"You're going to be the most grounded godlings in the history of the universe," Nana said. "We postponed handing out your punishment the last time you broke the rules. Give you an inch, and you go a mile."

"But, Nana!" Eli insisted. "We're the good guys, and we didn't break any rules this time."

"This is unwelcome news," Shangó said, settling on his throne next to Nana. By day, he was our science teacher, aka Mr. Jenkins, at Jackson Middle School. "If Tyana Nulan is back in the human world, then the Lord of Shadows has already made his next move."

"We should dispose of her now," Ogun proclaimed. All six of General's eyes lit up with excitement. He was drooling like he would be glad to gnaw on Nulan's bones if given the chance.

"Our first priority is to find out *why* she's here." Nana raised her hand, and vines grew from the floor and snaked around a still-unconscious Nulan.

"Agree," Eshu said. "Tyana is a trusted servant of the Lord of Shadows. Her presence could prove useful."

Eli swiped at the sweat beading on his forehead. It was taking all his strength to hold the ghosts this long. Once Nana had completely entangled Nulan in her vines, he let them go. "Thank you, thank you," he whispered to them as they left one by one. A tall, lanky ghost affectionately patted him on his head before vanishing.

Eli had built relationships with ghosts eager to help defend our world once he told them what was at stake. Some of the other spirits wanted to be left alone to haunt houses and graveyards or old hospitals, and he respected their wishes.

Nana's vines pulled Nulan down into the cloud of darkness at our feet. "We'll deal with her later," she said, then she turned her attention back to us. "Well, you're here now, so you might as well witness the first celestial to arrive from the edges of the universe."

"She should be here any moment now," Oshun added. "The Mother of All Things."

"We've been waiting for the rest of the celestials to arrive since this summer," Eli whispered to Eleni. "The council has refused to move against the Lord of Shadows until then."

"I've never met any of the celestials who dwelled beyond earth," Eleni said excitedly.

"You will today," Eshu interrupted their conversation, not bothering to hide that he was eavesdropping. Not that one could be stealthy in front of all-powerful gods or anything.

Deep down, I had hoped that it would be Oya, the orisha from my comic books. According to Papa, some of her children had started writing stories about her after she set off for a mission in outer space. She'd been gone for fifty years, which for a celestial was barely any time at all. But Oya wasn't the "mother of all things"; she was the warrior goddess, a protector with the fury of a storm when fighting for justice.

The fireflies in the ceiling nervously fluttered and their light pulsed brighter, then dimmer, then brighter again, until they suddenly went dark. The air grew colder around us.

I looked to the council, but they were frozen in place. Completely still. My heart sped up as I raised my staff. Something was wrong. The orishas' skin turned from their glowing, semi-divine states to dull gray. Then I knew.

"No!" Eleni cried out. "This can't be happening."

My mouth was dry when I finally croaked out my next words. "He's here . . . The Lord of Shadows, he's . . ."

"Not yet, Maya" came Captain Nulan's sickly sweet

voice. She rose from where Nana had buried her within a nest of vines. "But he will be soon."

We'd walked right into her trap. "You wanted us to bring you to the gods' realm."

Nulan smiled. "You've made things rather easy for me so far."

Eli balled his hands into fists as he flickered in and out of sight. He was trying to draw his ghosts back to him, but his energy was already spent, and none came. "Undo whatever you just did to Nana and the others."

Nulan shook her wings, and the vines still draped around her fell in a heap at her feet. A shadow shot out from her and caught Eli. He screamed, and as he did, the color faded from his face. "My lord has gifted me with a mere morsel of his powers. Enough so that I could trap the celestials. Do you think you, a mere godling, can challenge me, boy?"

"Let him go!" Frankie said through gritted teeth as she launched two balls of crackling electricity at Nulan.

This time, Nulan raised one hand, and the balls stopped in midair, halfway between her and us, then they dissipated. "Nice try."

I pivoted around and struck the shadow holding Eli with my staff. It hissed and dropped him. The color seeped back into his face. Once I saw my friend was okay, I turned on Nulan, the staff glowing. The symbols peeled off and flew at her. She tried to stop them, but there were too many, and one after another, they hit her, burning into her skin.

"By the way, Auntie," Eleni said with a twisted smile. "You're not the only one with tricks up your sleeves." Two separate gateways opened in the gods' realm. "I called for backup *again*."

I was slack-jawed, realizing that Eleni could open two gateways at the same time. I had to learn that trick and pronto.

Papa stepped out of one gateway, and the sky god, Obatala, stepped out of the other. Light pulsed around both celestials, and wind blew Papa's long locs across his face. "You should've stayed in the Dark world," he said, his voice a great echo. I could feel his power rolling off him in waves. Nulan grimaced, her skin still smoking from where the god symbols had burned into her.

"And you should've died there," she spat.

"Enough of this treachery," Obatala snapped. Sky Father appeared as a small man with ice-white eyes and white hair set against brown skin. "Let's see how the Lord of Shadows fares without you sowing despair in the human world." God symbols formed chains around Nulan's wrists and ankles. She pushed against them, but it was no use. At that, Obatala vanished with Nulan back into the gateway. I assumed that he was taking her to Azur, the city in the clouds.

With Nulan gone, Papa turned to Eleni and me. He had

looked brave only a moment ago, but his face creased into worry lines now. "Are you okay?" he asked. "Did she hurt you?"

Eli brushed at his jacket like the shadow had left dirt behind. "She caught me off guard, but I'm okay." Frankie rolled her eyes at him.

"Great heavens," Nana said as she and the other celestials began to stir again on their thrones. "Ogun, you were right. We should have disposed of her."

Eleni walked over to Papa, and he pulled her into a hug. I knew this was harder for her. Nulan was her auntie and had betrayed their whole family. I joined them on Papa's opposite side, and Eleni reached for my hand. Both Papa and I held her as she began to weep.

I didn't think for one minute that stopping Nulan would put an end to the Lord of Shadows' plans. If he could share his powers with her, we could expect more unpleasant surprises.

FIVE

LET'S TRY THIS AGAIN . . . THE FIRST CELESTIAL

AS SILVER FAIRY dust floated around Eleni, a wave of sadness settled over me. My whole body ached. It felt like the weight of the world was on my shoulders, but there was also this new hopelessness that I had never experienced before and a grave sense of loss.

How could we ever defeat the Lord of Shadows? He was too strong—too clever. I bit my lip, trying desperately to shake off my negative thoughts. We could beat him if we worked together and Papa, Eleni, and I figured out how to permanently repair the veil. I noticed Eli sniffling and Frankie reaching under her glasses to wipe her eyes, and I frowned. Why were we all suddenly so sad?

"What will Obatala do with Auntie Tyana?" Eleni asked as tears clustered on her eyelashes.

"Knowing Sky Father, he will take her to Alsar, the high-security prison for magical creatures who commit horrible crimes," Papa answered. "She won't hurt anyone else there."

"Good," Eleni said. "She deserves to be punished."

Papa reached out to catch flakes of her fairy dust. "Be careful, baby girl."

Eleni's eyes went wide as she looked at me, Eli, and Frankie. Then it all clicked. My friends and I were feeling her emotions, her sadness. I remembered a story that Papa once told me about the aziza. Their fairy dust had the ability to affect other people's moods and influence their decisions. The aziza had used their magic to keep strangers from invading their forest by making them think it was too dangerous to explore.

"Sorry, I didn't mean to do that!" Eleni apologized, ducking her head in embarrassment. She took a deep breath as if to calm herself, and the fairy dust disappeared. "I didn't know that I *could*. Kimala was the one good with fairy magic."

Papa stiffened at the mention of Kimala, like he always did when Eleni bought up her siblings or her mom. It might have been a long time ago, but Papa still missed them. As much as I'd been shocked to find out that he had another family before Mama and me, I could understand that the pain of losing them would never go away. Papa squeezed

Eleni tighter against his side. He looked like he wanted to say something but he held her instead.

Ogun cleared his throat. "I'll add another lesson on controlling one's magic to my lesson plan this week."

Back in the day—like earlier this year, right after school let out for the summer—most of the other godlings didn't even know they were related to celestials. They hadn't shown any magical abilities, and the orisha council had forbidden the other celestials from revealing the truth. Sound familiar? The council had a knack for rules, especially around magic. That was until the darkbringers started to attack our neighborhood and godlings started to show powers.

The cranky Johnston twins had once explained that the same thing had happened before the last war with the Dark. Godlings who'd lived ordinary lives started to come into their magic. It was like the universe could sense the need for the godlings to help the celestials protect the human world.

"It's time to go home," Papa said, looking us over. "You've been through enough today."

"But, Papa, the council said the first celestial will arrive from the outer edges of the universe soon," Eleni said, bouncing on her toes. "Can't we stay a little longer?"

"I'm already here," cooed a voice that sounded like crashing waves. "I've been observing and deliberating." Suddenly a spurt of water rose from the floor, quickly taking the shape of a person swathed in brilliant blue silk that flowed around them like an ocean.

When the celestial's form settled, she was a beautiful woman with deep brown skin, wearing a blue headscarf trimmed in silver and necklaces of cowrie shells. I recognized her from *Oya: Warrior Goddess* as the mother of the orishas. To clarify, she was the mother of almost all of the orishas and the protector of rivers and oceans.

"Yemoja," I said, breathless, amazed by her beauty.

"Why, yes, little one," Yemoja answered with a thoughtful expression like she was considering what to make of me. "You know me through my children." She glanced over at the celestials on their thrones: first at Shangó and Ogun, then Oshun. "I miss gazing upon your lovely faces."

Oshun squared her shoulders. She was practically glowing. "Thank the heavens you're here."

"It's been a long time," Shangó said.

Yemoja smiled broadly. "Nearly two thousand years."

"Time is a slippery thing," Ogun said, stroking General's huge, hairy back. "And now I fear we have very little of it to waste. This world is in grave danger."

Yemoja looked to Papa. "Elegguá, old friend, I can sense the distress of the veil. It must be a great burden to keep it intact."

"We're helping keep it up!" Eleni volunteered.

"And who are you, little one?" Yemoja asked.

"That's my sister, Eleni, and I'm Maya," I answered

protectively. "We're guardians of the veil in training, and these are our friends, Frankie and Eli."

"You precious little children," Yemoja said, her eyes welling with tears. "You deserve a better world than what you've inherited. It seems that the past is destined to repeat itself, but not to worry—we'll protect you as best as we can." Yemoja turned back to the other celestials. "Nana Buruku, you have done your job well leading this council. Now that I have returned, the five of you will relinquish your authority to me."

Say what? I caught Eli's and Frankie's eyes; they both looked confused. Was Yemoja dethroning the orisha council? Could she do that?

"Excuse me," Eli spoke up, "but no one bosses my grandmother around. She runs this place, and even though she can be a little strict sometimes, she's been doing a good job."

"Hush, boy," Nana said quickly, but her voice sounded gentler than usual, less snappy. "Yemoja, with all due respect, this council has worked for generations to build and protect this sanctuary. Most of the godlings under our protection only just learned of our existence. A change in leadership will cause panic."

"They will adjust," Yemoja said as the gods' realm began to change from a starry night to a bright, sunny day. The fireflies disappeared, replaced by rays of buttery yellow sunlight. Water and seafoam as fluffy as marshmallows began to whoosh around our ankles, warm and inviting.

The council members—Nana, Shangó, Ogun, Eshu, and Oshun—reluctantly stood up from their thrones. I thought they would've put up a fight, but they just stepped down from the raised platform in resignation.

"Papa, why are they listening to her?" I whispered. "She doesn't even know what's going on."

"Yemoja is one of the founding members of the original council," Papa explained, his voice low, though we both knew that everyone could hear us. "Her decision supersedes that of individual council members who are responsible for their neighborhood."

Yemoja snapped her fingers. "Enough small talk."

The five orisha thrones melted together and transformed into a throne made of seashells. Golden fish splashed around it, and a fan of water arched across the back more beautiful than Buckingham Fountain in Grant Park. "Once my counterparts arrive, we will do what we should have done before: we must rid ourselves of the entire Dark world."

I blinked, not quite registering what she was saying. She wanted to destroy *all* of the Dark. That would mean everyone: Zeran's little brother, the people who disagreed with the Lord of Shadows, and the ones who he'd brainwashed into following him.

"We must be swift," Ogun said. "Strike while we still have the chance."

"I fear it's our only course of action," Eshu said reluctantly.

"For once, we're in agreement," Oshun added.

Nana shook her head. "I'm not so sure."

"Nor am I." Shangó frowned. "There still might be a way to stop the Lord of Shadows."

"You can't be serious!" I blurted out. My voice was a sharp note, and everyone stared at me. I swallowed hard and tried to explain. "You can't destroy an entire world—all those people. How would we be any better than the Lord of Shadows?"

Yemoja leaned forward on her throne. The fish stopped splashing in the water around her feet. "How peculiar—you are a guardian in training, yet you are a champion of the Dark? Things really have changed since I have been gone."

"We went to the Dark twice," I said. "Not everyone wants a war with our world. We can't just ignore that. We even have a friend from the Dark who helped us escape the Lord of Shadows."

"Interesting." Yemoja ran her hand across a waterspout like it was a pet viper. "Elegguá, return the children to the human world. I will speak with Nana Buruku and the others in private. It seems that I have a lot to catch up on since my absence."

I didn't miss the way Yemoja talked with absolute authority. It wasn't *Elegguá, can you please return the children to the human world?* It was *Elegguá, return the children to the human world.* It was a not-so-subtle command that said that Yemoja was the new big boss. I got the feeling that with her now in control of the council, things were about to change around here.

"But we know the most about the Dark," I insisted, as Papa started to gather us to leave. "My friends and I have been there recently. We can tell you what we learned." I didn't want to be left out, not after everything we'd done to help protect our neighborhood and the human world.

Yemoja smiled brightly. "If I should require your assistance, you'll be the first to know."

I got the feeling that she would be even stricter than the orisha council. I wanted to tell her so much now about the Dark, Captain Nulan, and the Lord of Shadows.

One thing was for sure, we might have captured Nulan, but that couldn't be the end of it. It was *still* too easy. I would stake my entire Oya comic book collection that something *else* was going on—and I intended to find out with or without Yemoja's blessing.

SIX

It helps to get some fresh air

PAPA OPENED A gateway back to the community center, but he didn't come with us. Instead, he stayed to deliberate with the ex–council members and Yemoja. When we stepped out of the broom closet, we startled several people headed toward the main hall. It was bingo night, and the community center was hopping with the usual big shots.

Chief among them was Ms. Nichelle, the reigning champ and head of the Sassy Grandmas club. She screwed her face up into a disapproving scowl when she saw us. "What are you children doing in that closet? You better not be up to no good."

"Don't worry, Ms. Nichelle," Eli said with a winning smile. "If we were up to no good, you'll be the first to tell the whole neighborhood."

"Watch your mouth, Eli, before I tell your grandmother you were in a closet with not one but three girls," Ms. Nichelle threatened. "What do you think she'll say about that?"

"We weren't doing anything we weren't supposed to," Frankie said.

"Of course not," Ms. Nichelle droned, her eyes suddenly glazed over and her voice robotic. "You're good children."

"Shouldn't you be getting to the hall?" Eli quirked an eyebrow. "I'm sure your fellow *sassy* grandmas are waiting for you."

"Yes." Ms. Nichelle abruptly turned on her heels and walked away.

I snapped my head around to Eleni, who wasn't even paying attention to the conversation. Fairy dust floated around her, and she looked distracted as she chewed on her bottom lip.

"Eleni," I whispered. "Be careful . . . your magic!"

The last of the fairy dust faded when Ms. Nichelle was out of sight.

"Oh no!" Eleni jumped, horrified. "Sorry, I'm having a hard time controlling it."

"How can you open multiple gateways at once and be so bad at your fairy magic?" I crossed my arms. "It defies logic."

Maybe I was being unfair, but she couldn't just go

around bewitching people like that, especially defenseless humans like Ms. Nichelle, who had no clue about magic.

"She's not bad at her fairy magic," Eli said, taking Eleni's side. "She's just coming into those powers, so you should give her a break. You know what it was like when you first tried to open a gateway."

I cringed. He meant what it was still like. Yes, I was better at opening gateways, but I was much slower than Papa and Eleni, and I couldn't open more than one at a time. I was also notoriously slow when closing tears in the veil without my staff. So yeah, I knew what it was like. I let out a shaky breath. "All I'm saying is that we have to be careful with our magic in front of humans."

"I don't see how that matters with the impending war with the Dark," Eli countered. "Let's not forget the fact that darkbringers are already running around our world. Do you think they care about showing themselves to humans?"

"I would argue that they *do* care," Frankie said after clearing her throat. "Had the darkbringers been reckless and revealed themselves left and right, we'd have heard about it by now. They have a bigger plan. That's why the Lord of Shadows sent Captain Nulan."

The music flared up in the bingo hall, and a man's voice blasted over the speakers. "Everybody clap your hands. Clap, clap, clap, clap your hands. Clap, clap, clap, clap your hands. All right now, we're going to do the basic step."

Ms. Nichelle and her friends lined up to do the cha-cha slide just as Eli's auntie shuffled into the hallway with his little sister, Jayla, who had her curly hair in two pigtails. "Eli!" Jayla exclaimed as she ran to hug him. "Where are your ghosts?"

"Haven't I already told you that there are no such things as ghosts?" their auntie chided her. "Eli, you have to stop filling her head with nonsense." Auntie Bae was their great-aunt on their human side and knew nothing about magic or otherworldly things.

"They're just stories," Eli said, winking at Jayla.

Jayla winked back, contorting half of her face to close one eye. "Yeah, just STORIES!"

Auntie Bae shook her head and entered the hall, where the cha-cha slide was in full swing now. "Slide to the left, slide to the left," the song blasted on the loudspeaker. "All right now, this is my jam," she said as she joined the sliders.

Eli cracked his knuckles. "Jayla and I have bingo to officiate."

Jayla tried to crack her knuckles, too. "Let's do this!"

"You are the coolest little sister ever," Eli said, giving her a fist bump.

Jayla giggled in delight as the two of them headed toward the bingo hall.

Eleni, Frankie, and I left the community center and entered into the frigid Chicago winter. The cold air hit my lungs, but it felt refreshingly normal, and I needed normal right now. A giant snowman sat on the lawn in front of the main building, and icicles covered the trees along the street. It was hard to believe that after finishing up training with Ogun, we'd been to a garbage dump halfway across the country and to the gods' realm, all before nightfall.

"How are we going to figure out what Nulan was up to?" I wondered out loud.

"Does it matter now if she's in Alsar?" Eleni asked. "She can't do harm there."

Frankie frowned as we picked our way through a fresh foot of snow on the sidewalk. "What do you know about Alsar?"

"Not much," Eleni said quietly. "Only that it's a prison run by the Azurian peacekeepers."

"Charlie told me that my orisha mom was a peace-keeper." Frankie stuffed her hands in her pockets and drew in a shaky breath. "Maybe someone there might remember who she was searching for before she . . . *you know*. I already asked the orisha council, and they said that they don't get involved in Azurian affairs. So maybe the other peacekeep-ers might know."

Charlie was a two-faced kishi, meaning he literally had two faces. He had a human face on the front of his head, though a very hairy one, and on the backside, a hyena face with yellow eyes and sharp teeth. We met him at the start of the school year when Papa took us to see Sky Father. We'd been in a crowded market, and Charlie thought that Frankie was her orisha mom because they looked so much alike. He told us that Frankie's mom was the head peacekeeper in Azur for centuries. She hunted down rogue magical creatures across the universe. Most were out to seed chaos or incite wars.

I rocked on my heels when we reached the intersection. Frankie's house was three blocks east, and our house was two blocks north. "Maybe you should talk to Charlie again," I suggested.

"He hasn't been answering my calls." Frankie stared down at her boots. "He said he would help, but so far, he's been ghosting me."

"He's wrong for that," I said, annoyed. "I knew we couldn't trust him. Kishis are always tricksters. Well, at least they are in the stories." I sighed. "Sorry, that's not right. The fact is Charlie broke his promise."

"I'm good at finding stuff on the internet," Eleni volunteered. "Maybe I'll uncover a lead."

Frankie glanced across her shoulder, looking longingly in the direction of home. "I hope you have better luck than I've had so far."

"As for Nulan, let's start asking around to see if any of the other godlings have heard anything suspicious sounding," I suggested. "I'll talk to Tisha Thomas tomorrow at school. She has the gift of foresight, so maybe she's seen something useful."

"If the celestials didn't know what Auntie Tyana was doing here, then how will we figure it out?" Eleni asked.

That was the million-dollar question, and I had a zero-dollar answer. "I don't know yet."

After we parted ways with Frankie, we saw Miss Lucille taking groceries from the back seat of her and Miss Ida's red sedan. I mean, the twins didn't need to go shopping, but they liked the human side of their lives. That was why they were so fussy about their prized tulips, which they grew without magic. Right now, there weren't any tulips in their yard, just piles of snow.

It was still hard to believe that Miss Lucille, her twin, Miss Ida, and my sister were technically around the same age. Well, Eleni was about a thousand and fourteen, while the twins were two thousand years old, give or take a few decades.

"Have you seen Zeran?" Miss Lucille asked, juggling three paper bags. "My sister said he wasn't home yet. He's supposed to help her with dinner."

Eleni looked at me, and I resisted the urge to shrug. So much for strawberry cheesecake. "We got separated at the community center," I said, not exactly fibbing. "You know how it gets down there on bingo night."

"Maybe I should go fetch him before it gets too

crowded," Miss Lucille said.

She wasn't going to find Zeran there, which only brought up more questions. Where was he? Who else did he know on this side of the veil besides the cranky twins and us? There were the other darkbringers who'd snuck into the human world, plotting to carry out orders from the Lord of Shadows, but if he was secretly meeting with them . . . then that would mean . . . it would mean that Tisha Thomas's vision was true. I swallowed hard.

"I'll get those bags, Miss Lucille," Zeran said, stepping out of the shadows.

Miss Lucille frowned at him. He'd clearly come from the opposite direction of the community center.

"I went for a walk to clear my head," he explained before she asked. He gave me a sidelong glance, then looked away guiltily. "I have a lot on my mind."

"It helps to get some fresh air." Miss Lucille smiled sadly as she handed him the grocery bags. "I know living here is a big transition, especially with worrying about your brother."

Zeran said nothing as he and Miss Lucille headed inside. That was when I noticed the mud and grass caked on his boots. All the grass in Chicago had long since withered and retreated underneath the snow. He'd traveled someplace far, like farther than the Midwest, to have that much grass on his shoes this time of the year.

Eleni let out a deep sigh. "Poor Zeran. I can't imagine

what it was like for him to leave his brother behind."

The kernel of doubt I had earlier was nagging at me. I had gotten to know Zeran pretty well over the last few months. He wanted nothing more than to save his brother, Billu, from a life with the darkbringer army. He'd even defied his father, Commander Rovey, gotten himself locked up in a cage, and helped us raid the Crystal Palace in hopes of finding his brother.

Zeran wasn't one to give up. He was more stubborn than me. If he had a way to rescue his brother, he'd take it, even if it meant betraying us. Deep down, I wondered if I would do the same for Mama, Papa, Eleni, or one of my friends, but I already knew the answer.

SEVEN

DARK SIDE

ONCE WE WERE inside our house, Eleni and I stepped into the hallway and slipped out of our sneakers. I inhaled a shaky breath as I hung my coat on the hook beside the door. The house smelled like vanilla and sugar and Mama's lilac perfume. It smelled like *home*. I couldn't let the Lord of Shadows take this away from me. Papa, Mama, Eleni, and me . . . we had a good life. We had friends and neighbors who we cared about and who cared about us. The human world might've had its faults, but it was the only home we knew.

Mama appeared at the edge of the living room wearing green oven mitts and a yellow apron over her scrubs. She had her hair pulled up into a puffy ponytail. "What *is* that smell?"

"Decomposing trash baked in the sun," I said innocently.

"The good news is that we delivered my evil auntie to the orisha council for punishment," Eleni added.

Mama pulled off her mitts and apron with a deep sigh. She shook her head. "I'm going to be gray before my time, raising two godlings."

"Two guardians in training," I said proudly.

Mama smiled. "Two brilliant, beautiful girls who will do well on their exams next week because they've been making time to study, *correct*?"

"Yes, ma'am!" Eleni answered cheerily while I groaned.

I was still getting used to Eleni calling Mama *ma'am*. But what else would she call her? Certainly not Clarisse or Mrs. Abeola. It wasn't something that we'd ever talked about.

"So does your father know about this evil auntie?" Mama asked.

"I'm afraid so." Eleni grimaced. "He and Obatala helped us stop her."

Mama wrung the apron and mitts in her hands. "I guess it was too much to hope that the Lord of Shadows would climb back under a rock and leave us alone."

"Maybe when pigs can fly," I said. Scratch that: they probably already could. "Actually, not even then."

"I won't stand in your way of guarding the veil, but I

want you both to promise me that you'll stay safe and won't take any unnecessary risks," Mama said. "Leave the Lord of Shadows to the celestials, okay?"

I cocked my head to the side. "Define *unnecessary*."

Mama gave me a look serious enough to make chocolate melt and onions cry. She didn't have to say another word.

"You know what?" I gulped down a mouthful of air. "Never mind."

"We'll be extra careful," Eleni said, glancing at me. "We have each other now."

"You're still only kids." Mama cleared her throat. "Try to keep that in mind."

Once Mama left for work, Eleni announced, "No offense, Maya, but you stink."

To think that she'd been the one rolling around in garbage soup and she had the nerve to tell me that I smelled bad. The hypocrisy of it all.

***

The next morning, I forced myself to climb out of bed before daybreak after tossing and turning all night. What was Captain Nulan's mission in the human world? Was she here to recruit magical creatures like Eleni suggested? Was she doing reconnaissance on the orishas? Did she have a plan to bring the veil down faster? She sure wasn't sightseeing or trying out the local cuisine.

Eleni was right about one thing: Nulan couldn't do

anything now that she was imprisoned in Alsar. But whatever the Lord of Shadows was planning, he'd find a way to do it without her. He had plenty of cronies willing to help him.

I rubbed my eyes, second-guessing myself. I wanted to crawl back underneath my blanket and sleep until it was time to go to school. I groaned as I fought the urge. Did I mention that I am not a morning person?

Feeling restless, I slipped into warm clothes, grabbed my staff, and crept down the stairs. No one was up yet. I needed something to do—anything to burn off my nervous energy. I pulled on my boots and stepped into the backyard. It was covered in a fresh layer of snow, perfect and untouched. Our neighbor's dog, Lucky, pressed his face against the window to stare at me. The golden retriever wagged his tail excitedly. At least someone was happy to be awake this early.

I had to get faster at opening gateways. Eleni had been asleep for a thousand years, and she still understood her godling magic better than me. *Well, mostly.* She was still accidentally enchanting people. That said, she made an excellent guardian in training. She could not only open a gateway at the snap of her fingers, but she could open multiple gateways at once. Maybe it was different with her because she was half celestial and half aziza. She had magic from both sides. I had to up my game.

"I've got this," I said, hyping myself.

As I tightened my grip on the staff, the symbols glowed one by one against the morning fog: the sun, a leopard with raised paws, and a river. *I am the guardian of the veil.* Sometimes I didn't feel like a guardian, not when I had unknowingly let the Lord of Shadows trick me into permanently damaging the only thing that protected our world from his wrath.

"Thanks for the vote of confidence, buddy," I said to the staff, and it glowed ever brighter as the other symbols began to pulse. "But I can't always rely on you to channel my powers." Like my math teacher, Ms. Vanderbilt, would say, *Practice makes perfect.* Though she was talking about algebra, it was time to put that to the test.

I set the staff on the porch, in a spot safe from the snow. The wind whipped across my face, and my teeth chattered, but I pushed that distraction aside. I focused on the space between the backyard and the garage. "It's now or never."

There were two ways to travel across great distances. One was via a gateway, which made the speed of light seem like moving in slow motion. You could get to places fast, but not instantly. If I wanted to get from point A, let's say the backyard, to point B, let's say Azur, at almost the exact same moment in time, I needed a wormhole. A wormhole bent space like folding a sheet of paper, so the two points were side by side.

Wormholes were trickier to make because you could

accidentally destroy a planet or a whole galaxy if you didn't know what you were doing. Even Eleni had never tried to bend space. I would be sticking to gateways, thank you very much.

I was thinking of this when the first sparks of magic appeared in front of me. The shorter the gateway, the easier it was to make, so I concentrated on opening the other end in my room. The sparks grew and transformed into a roaring black hole in thirty seconds. Not bad. But when I attempted to open a second gateway, the first one abruptly closed. I groaned in frustration.

The second gateway had opened in Daniel Boone National Forest in Kentucky and had taken close to a minute to make. I figured no one would see it and freak out this early in the morning. I could smell the pine needles and wet grass in the breeze.

I closed my eyes and tried to open another gateway. There were no sparks of magic or roaring black hole this time, but I felt something vast and hollow. Whispers echoed in my ears. Hundreds of them. It was like being in an auditorium right before Principal Ollie took the mic and every kid was talking over each other.

"What are you doing, baby girl?" Papa said from behind me.

Startled, I let go of the magic maintaining the gateway, and it snapped shut. The whispers also stopped. Had I imagined them? "I thought I could practice some more, so I'm better at opening gateways," I told Papa. "But I'm failing miserably."

"You only learned what a gateway was a few months ago," he said, coming to a stop next to me. "Since then, you rescued your old man twice, and you call that failure?"

I glanced down at my snow-caked boots. "I also let the Lord of Shadows trick me. Not to mention that I'm slow when fixing holes in the veil without my staff. Eleni is a better guardian in training."

"Is that what you're worried about—that Eleni is better than you?" Papa's eyebrows pinched together. "Maya, no two people are the same. It's not about being as good as someone else or better than them. Always do your best. That's all any of us can do. Sometimes we fall short, and that's okay."

"It's not okay when the world is at stake." I blew out a frustrated breath. "I can't keep falling short when everyone needs me."

"Last time I checked, you're not by yourself, baby girl." Papa squeezed my shoulder. "Sometimes there are things you can change on your own, but sometimes, if people want to change things—especially something really big—we have to do it together. You, Eleni, me, the other celestials and godlings, if we want a better world, then we have to make it ourselves." Papa looked down at me, his eyes filled with light. "And as for feeling bad that the Lord of Shadows tricked you, you're a kid, Maya, and he's an adult. If anyone should be feeling bad and ashamed, it should be him."

I leaned against Papa. The backyard had gone silent without the roaring sound of the gateway, except for Lucky whining in the window next door. Poor thing. He looked like he wanted to get outside badly.

"I think it's good if I keep practicing," I said. "I still want to be better."

"Of course—it's important for you to understand the extent of your godling powers, but be careful," Papa said. "I came out here this morning because I felt you opening a gateway beyond this galaxy."

"Really?" I said in shock as I remembered the strange sensation and the whispers.

"There are some places that are too dangerous to visit, places of pure chaos," explained Papa. "The Lord of Shadows may be a threat to *this* world and galaxy, but he is not the only one. Thankfully there is no way for the chaos to reach here as long as we do not let it in."

I shuddered at the idea that there were things more dangerous than the Lord of Shadows, but I supposed that I should have guessed it. Mental note: be careful where I open my next gateway.

"Papa, Yemoja can't really be serious about destroying the Dark," I said. "That's wrong on so many levels that I don't know where to start."

Papa took a beat too long to answer as he stared at the snow. "The councils across all the sanctuaries have been debating that option for the better part of a millennium," he finally said. "Some believe that it is an acceptable loss to protect the rest of the universe."

I swallowed hard. "What do you believe?"

Papa's shoulders sank as he turned to me. "Two wrongs don't make a right. Like you said, if we destroy the Dark world, then we're no better than the Lord of Shadows."

"We have to convince her to change her mind."

"She seems to have taken your words to heart," Papa said. "For now, she's holding on the attack. She's planning to discuss it at a meeting with all the councils tomorrow before proceeding."

That was a relief for the time being, but not by much. We had enough to worry about without the celestials turning all *dark side*. Maybe if we could find out what the Lord of Shadows was planning, Yemoja and the other celestials could come up with another way to stop him before they decided to destroy the Dark.

EIGHT

WANT TO KNOW THE FUTURE?

BY THE TIME I got dressed for school, Eleni was on her second batch of waffles smothered in apple preserves. She and Papa had made the concoction last month, and it tasted better than apple pie. "There you are finally," Eleni said, stuffing her mouth. "I'm surprised that you were up before me."

I dropped into the chair across from her. "I'll try not to make it a habit."

"I love watching the sunrise," Eleni said in her singsong voice. "It's my favorite part of the day. Well, when we can see the sun here, which admittedly isn't that often this time of the year."

As Papa set a plate of fresh waffles in front of me, he raised one eyebrow. When I frowned, he jerked his head toward Eleni. "Maya was practicing this morning," he said leadingly.

Eleni beamed like a light bulb had gone off. "Maybe we can practice together. You can work on your gateways while I figure out how to control my fairy magic, so I can stop enchanting people by mistake. What do you think?"

That actually didn't sound like a bad idea. I was so busy worrying about how much better she was with gateways, but we were both still learning our magic. So were Frankie and Eli and the rest of the godlings.

By the time we headed out the door for school, Zeran was leaning against our gate. His hoodie covered most of his face, and he didn't meet either of our eyes. Eleni cast me a look and nudged my shoulder.

"Um . . . Zeran," I said awkwardly. "How was your little stroll around the neighborhood yesterday?"

"Fine," he answered stiffly, as we started for school.

"*Fine*? You rushed out of the community center like it was so important," I pressed.

Zeran groaned. "I'm getting really tired of you poking your nose in my business, Maya."

I cocked my head to the side. "And what business is that?"

"Nothing that concerns you," he shot back.

"Well, in case you forgot, we're on the brink of war with the Dark right now," I said, losing my patience with him.

"So a lot more concerns me than you might think."

"Just drop it, Maya." Zeran rubbed his forehead. "I'm not in the mood."

"I think we should keep talking," I said. "You've been acting weird for weeks."

Zeran turned to Eleni. "Why is your sister as stubborn as an impundulu?"

Eleni's eyes went wide as she looked back and forth between the two of us. She didn't dare agree with him but also, she didn't *not* agree with him either. "Um . . ."

"Did you just call me a giant killer bird?" I asked, offended but also sort of pleased with myself. If I was going to be compared to a magical creature, it might as well be one that most people had enough sense not to mess with.

"In addition to being nosy, you're very single-minded when you want something," Zeran said. "So, yes, in that way, you're just like an impundulu."

"I'd rather be single-minded than think I know everything like you."

Zeran smiled. "So you admit that you're single-minded?"

"Only if you admit to being a know-it-all," I said, crossing my arms.

Zeran shrugged when we reached Eli's house. "I guess we're at an impasse."

Catching the tail end of our conversation, Eli said, "Oh look, they're fighting again—a surprise to absolutely no one."

I grimaced, annoyed. "No we're not."

"Definitely not," Zeran added. "Maya was just being nosy as usual."

I rolled my eyes. That's what I got for caring.

Eli laughed. "Keep this up and people will think you're more than friends."

"What?" Zeran said.

"Don't be ridiculous," I snapped.

Eli and Eleni exchanged a secret glance. What was that all about? Gross. Maybe some of the other kids at school swooned over Zeran because he had wings and he was blue and all, but not me. I had better things to do.

The rest of the way to Frankie's house was awkward until Eli started talking about his favorite internet show, *Ghost Sightings*. "Get this. Al and Carl Davis, the head ghosthunters, have gotten tons of messages these last few weeks. They've estimated a thousand percent increase in ghost activity across the globe. That can't be a coincidence with what's happening with the veil. The ghosts are all revved up."

Eleni wrapped her arms around her shoulders. "It was like this last time, too—a flurry of unusual occurrences. I remember the Bigfoot clans fleeing the mountains and the merfolk leaving their seas in droves. They were looking for safe havens."

"There are no safe havens from the Lord of Shadows," I said. I didn't want to be the bearer of bad news, but we all knew it. None of us would be able to hide from his wrath against the human world if we didn't stop him.

As Frankie dashed out the door and we continued to school, I didn't want to think about the Lord of Shadows invading our world or the possibility that Zeran could be a spy. I didn't want to worry about people getting hurt or more fighting. I wanted to walk to school with my friends, teasing each other instead of talking about the end of the world.

"Frankie, I found something interesting," Eleni said as she pulled a slip of paper from her pocket. "On the morning your mother disappeared, she stopped at a farmers' market in South Loop, right on the edge of downtown. One of the news stations was reporting on the market at the same time and snapped this photo."

We all gathered around as Eleni unfolded the paper and handed it to Frankie. The picture was of a crowd of people walking through tables of vegetables, fruits, homemade cakes, and jars of honey. It wasn't hard to spot Frankie's orisha mom. Even in her human form, she radiated this natural light around her. Now I understood why the kishi Charlie had mistaken Frankie for her mom. They both were tall with dark brown skin, dark eyes, and high cheekbones.

Frankie's hands shook as she stared down at the image. "She was so beautiful."

"Like you," I said, and Frankie smiled at me with tears in her eyes.

"Do you see those three in the background?" Eleni pointed out a woman and two men. They looked ordinary and fit in with the crowd at first glance, but the more I stared at them, the more the picture seemed to change. The woman's image blurred so you couldn't make out her face. One of the men looked like a bodybuilder, and the other had tentacles poking out from around the sleeves of his jacket.

Eli cleared his throat. "That's creepy."

"Are they darkbringers?" I asked, rocking on my heels.

Zeran grimaced as he, too, stared at the photo. "No."

"How do you know for sure?" I asked.

"Call it a gut feeling," he replied.

"I agree." Frankie bit her lip. "Charlie said that my celestial mom had been on earth to hunt down rogue criminals from Azur, so it's more likely that these three come from there. I have to find out who they are."

"I'll help you," Eli volunteered.

"We all will," I added, and Frankie nodded.

When we arrived at Jackson Middle, kids were filing into the main building. Soon Eleni's friends from her eighth-grade class swept her into their ranks. I spotted

Tisha Thomas at a water fountain down the hall. "I'll catch up with you in homeroom," I said to my friends as I made a beeline for her. "Hey, Tisha, can I talk to you about something?"

Tisha looked up at me with eerie silver eyes. Her eyes hadn't been like that before she came into her godling powers, and now they had an otherworldly quality to them. "This wouldn't be a good place to have *that* conversation," she said. She had such a serene edge to her voice, almost dreamlike. "We have five minutes before homeroom starts."

"The lab." I pointed down the hall. Shangó, the orisha of lightning, aka Mr. Jenkins, our science teacher, was always in the lounge during homeroom, since he didn't have a class that period. The lab would be empty.

Tisha followed me inside, and the lights came on overhead. "You want to know how Zeran will betray you."

"No . . . um, yes." I shook my head. "But I wanted to ask you about Captain Nulan first."

Tisha frowned. "Who?"

"Tyana Nulan," I said, realizing that Tisha had no clue who I was talking about. "She works for the Lord of Shadows. I was just wondering if maybe you'd had a vision about her."

"Why would I have a vision about some random

person?" Tisha asked, confused.

This conversation was going nowhere fast. "Isn't that how it works?"

"I'm not quite sure how it works," Tisha admitted.

"You can read minds too, can't you?" I was not too fond of the idea that she could know all my secrets if she chose to dig deep enough. "You read my mind at the beginning of the school year and asked about the Dark."

"Sometimes." Tisha leaned against the blackboard and massaged her forehead. "I don't know all your secrets, nor do I want to know them. I can only read surface-level thoughts." Tisha suddenly glared at me. "I'm not a liar!"

I grimaced. "I didn't say that."

"But you were thinking it," Tisha accused.

"There's a difference between thinking something and saying it." I glanced down at my shoelaces. I was disappointed that she couldn't tell me anything about Nulan, but it was a long shot to start with. "So . . . you think Zeran is going to betray me."

"That's what I saw." Tisha crossed her arms defensively. Not that I blamed her. I didn't mean to question her godling powers. "My mom says that people only think they want to know the future, but it's too big of a burden to bear when you can't do anything to change it."

"Are you saying once you see something, it will happen?"

"Yes," she whispered.

"Tell me," I insisted.

"I saw Zeran with two other darkbringers in an old factory by Thirty-Fifth and Ashland," Tisha explained, then her silver eyes started to glow. "One of the darkbringers said, 'If you want to save your brother, bring us the young guardian. The one they call Maya.'" Tisha paused, and her voice deepened. "'I'll deliver her when we meet next, then you'll tell me where to find Billu. Do we have a deal?'" Tisha glanced away. "I had another vision. You were unconscious and tied up in a sack while Zeran and another darkbringer stood over you."

I stared at Tisha, speechless. I hadn't expected her to give me a rundown. If Zeran had asked, I would have helped him find his little brother without a second thought. That was what friends did for each other. Instead, *according to Tisha*, at some point in the near future, he'll go straight to the darkbringers to offer me up in exchange for his brother. I was more than a little hurt.

Now I wasn't even sure that I wanted to confront him about it. Would he tell me the truth or lie to cover his tracks? Either way, it was going to be extremely unpleasant for both of us.

When the first bell rang, Tisha adjusted her Hello Kitty backpack. She gave me a sympathetic look before she turned on her heels and left the lab. She'd been right—or at least her mom had been when she'd warned her: people shouldn't know their futures, especially if there was nothing we could do about them. This really sucked.

NINE

A WORD OF ADVICE

I COULDN'T ACCEPT that there was nothing I could do to change what Tisha Thomas saw. Zeran *would* betray me, but he *hadn't* yet. If every action we made impacted the future, couldn't I convince him of another way to rescue his brother? I let out a frustrated sigh. This was an impossible situation.

"Well, this explains a lot about what's going on at JMS, Abeola," someone said from the far side of the lab. It wasn't just someone. It was Gail Galanis, the new girl from upstate New York who started at Jackson Middle this year. The same Gail who sported a different temporary tattoo on her forearm every week even though it was out of dress code. She was also in after-school math tutoring with me, even though she clearly didn't need the extra help. She just liked to show off. "I should've realized that you'd be at the center of the weirdness at school."

"You have no clue what you're talking about." I rolled my eyes as she lifted her head from a desk. I couldn't believe that she'd been here the whole time. "Also, news flash, eavesdropping on other people's conversation doesn't go over well here at JMS, not sure how things are in upstate New York."

"I wasn't eavesdropping." Gail yawned. "I was sleeping before you two rudely barged in and woke me up, gossiping about Zeran and all. So he's a darkbringer? I should have known he was too perfect to be true."

"We were not gossiping." Wait, hold up. Did she say he was *too perfect to be true*? "We were . . . *um* making stuff up for a play we're writing."

"You're an awful liar, Abeola," Gail said. "I know all about the Dark, the darkbringers, the Lord of Shadows."

"Is that so?" I mouthed. There were technically only two ways Gail could know the truth: one, she was a godling, or two, she was one of the rare humans who could see magic. "Please enlighten me."

"First of all, the godlings at school aren't very good at keeping secrets." Gail stretched her arms over her head in a calculated way that reminded me of a cat circling a mouse. "I hear them whispering about their new powers all the time. They also say things like, 'What happens if this Lord of Shadows really comes to our world?' 'He must not be too tough if Maya fought him and survived.' 'I bet he's a punk.' Stuff like that." Gail paused for dramatic effect. "You know?"

I laughed, and it was one sharp note. "You really shouldn't believe everything you hear."

"Cut the crap, Abeola," Gail said as she stood up. "I know your father is a celestial, and Eli's grandmother is one too. If I had to guess, probably a third of the kids at our school are godlings."

I crossed my arms. Part of me wanted to keep denying it, but it was clear that she already knew the truth. "Then you must know that the Lord of Shadows isn't a joke, and when he comes, the kids making fun of me will see that for themselves." After going into the Dark and squaring up against him twice, I still didn't get any respect at school. Not fair.

"Oh, you're admitting that it's all real, good." Gail slipped on a devious smile. "You're all right, Abeola. Another kid might have kept on lying about it."

"If the celestials find out you know their secret, they're going to erase your memories," I told her. "They're afraid that people will panic if the human world discovers the truth."

"I'm immune to magic." Gail waved her hand dismissively. "My cousin is a demigod and tried to turn my brother and me into toads when I was ten. It worked on my brother, but I was unaffected."

"Oh." I had so many questions. She had a demigod cousin, as in he was part god too? How was she immune to magic? Papa had told me there were celestials all over the world, representing every people and culture. "So your brother is a toad now?"

"My uncle turned him back into a pimple-faced brat, which is his usual state of being." Gail laughed and headed for the door as the second-to-last warning bell rang for first period.

"You can't tell anybody, especially the part about Zeran," I said, feeling uneasy. "It's . . . complicated, you know? I'm still trying to figure it out."

"A word of advice, Maya." Gail stopped and turned on her heels. "Demigods, or in your case godlings, can have very limited perspectives, especially if they have *the sight* like Tisha Thomas." Gail cupped her hands around the sides of her face. "Sometimes they only see what's right in front of them and not the whole picture."

I thought about what Gail meant. Tisha Thomas saw Zeran betray me in a warehouse sometime in the future. But she didn't know why or what happened to lead to Zeran offering me up to the darkbringers. Not that anything I would ever do should result in that level of betrayal, thank you very much.

At that, Gail and I slipped out of the science lab. She

jetted down the hall and stepped into her class right before the final bell rang. I wasn't as lucky.

"Miss Abeola, you're tardy," Ms. Taylor said as I entered first period. She opened a notebook on her desk and scribbled down my name. JMS had a strict code. For every three tardies, you got a day of detention—either regular detention or the yoga room, where you had to reflect on being a better student.

"Sorry, Ms. Taylor," I said, shrugging off my backpack and heading for my seat. Eli had the same first period as Tisha Thomas and Gail Galanis, but Zeran and Frankie were already at our table. Frankie was arranging her notepad next to a copy of *The Hill We Climb* by Amanda Gorman. To her left, Zeran leaned back in his chair, twirling his pencil between his fingers.

"The so-called guardian of the veil just walked in," Winston whispered to Candace and Tay, who unfortunately sat one row over from us. He had one of his hands under the table, where little blue flames danced on his fingertips. "More like the guardian of the forever losers club."

Usually, I would have had a comeback, but I didn't have the energy to deal with Winston and his cronies this morning. How could any of the celestials think they would ever lift a finger to help save our world from the Lord of Shadows?

Tay laughed at Winston's very unfunny joke, and their

table shook slightly. His godling power was to control seismic waves, but he didn't quite seem to have it under control.

"Will you cut that out?" Candace said, her nose in a chess book. "I can't think."

"You know there's such a thing as overpreparing," Tay said, dismissing her.

Winston slapped Candace on the back. "Chess queen of the Midwest."

Candace smiled, but she didn't stop looking in her book until Ms. Taylor announced, "Good morning, class! Don't forget that this week, we'll start voting for our winter break book club read. Get your picks in by Wednesday. I'll announce the winner on Friday."

I sank into the seat next to Frankie and tried and failed not to look at Zeran. He quirked an eyebrow as if to ask why I was staring at him, and I quickly turned away.

Zeran let out a frustrated sigh. "Are you still being weird?"

"No," I blurted out so quickly that it was obvious that I was, in fact, still being weird.

I attempted to focus as our English teacher dove into her lesson, but there was so much on my mind. Captain Nulan's appearance at the garbage dump. The arrival of Yemoja from the edges of the universe. Not to mention that she had disbanded the orisha council. Tisha Thomas's vision of Zeran delivering an unconscious me to the darkbringers.

Oh, and Gail Galanis could not only see magic, she was immune to it. Add all that to the fact that the veil was failing and the Lord of Shadows despised everything to do with the human world.

"So what do you think?" Frankie asked, her voice pitched low. Ms. Taylor carried on about the three-act structure in storytelling. She was saying something about setup, confrontation, and resolution. If I had to plop our lives into the three-act structure, I'd guess we were nearing the confrontation act if we couldn't figure out how to stop the Lord of Shadows.

"Huh?" I hadn't been entirely paying attention to either Frankie or Ms. Taylor.

"Going back to Azur." Frankie frowned. "I think we'll get more information about the people in the photo with my mom if we start there."

"I think it's a good idea," I said. Technically we could go during lunch. Time worked differently on Azur. We could be there for hours and only a few minutes would've passed on earth.

A crash rang out in the hallway outside of our classroom. "What the heck?"

Frankie glanced over my shoulder. "Oh no."

Zeran pushed back his chair so hard that the legs scraped across the floor. Ms. Taylor was standing still with one hand gesturing to the chalkboard. A cloud had fallen across the window, and the lights flickered overhead. All around us, our human classmates had frozen in place. Some were in the middle of passing notes, some listening to Ms. Taylor with glazed-over expressions, some looking sleepy eyed. But I hadn't gotten that usual tingling across my forearms when there was a tear in the veil.

"What did you do now, little Maya?" Winston spat. "I'm sure this is your fault."

Ignoring him, I jumped to my feet along with the rest of the godlings. "Darkbringers?"

Zeran morphed into his true form: winged, blue, horned. Someone squealed in delight at the back of the room, and I cringed. He nodded somberly. "Yup."

Sparks of energy crackled on Frankie's fingertips. Blue flames flickered on Winston's arms. Candace grew to twice her size, the chess book forgotten. Wind whipped through the room as another godling changed into something otherworldly. She floated in an aura of purple mist, and her skin had become almost translucent, her braids glimmering.

I slipped off my ring, and it turned back into a staff. "We have to protect the school."

Winston stormed to the door. "Maybe you got lucky in the Dark, but this is my neighborhood. Nobody's going to come in here and start something."

As soon as Winston stepped into the hallway, a black tentacle latched itself around his waist. "What the . . ." he growled as he hit the floor hard on his back. Tay and Candace were stunned as I pushed past them, but it was already too late. The tentacle dragged Winston, screaming, into the chaos.

The hall was swarming with darkbringers. Godlings were trying to fight them off and losing.

TEN

YOU MUST BE THE GHOST BOY

WINSTON LET OUT another high-pitched scream as the tentacle dragged him down the hall. He slammed into other godlings and darkbringers alike, taking some down with him. The fluorescent lights overhead flickered in and out until they died, plunging JMS into darkness. Sparks of magic lit up sporadically, revealing flashes of blue, barbed tails, curved horns, and wings. By my count, there had to be at least two dozen darkbringers in the hallway.

We learned months ago that darkbringers had been sneaking into our world through tears in the veil. There'd been so many tears that Papa, Eleni, and I couldn't close them fast enough. How many had crossed already? Hundreds, thousands, tens of thousands? The Lord of Shadows had a sleeper army right under our noses. Was that why Nulan had come—to join them? The bigger question was, why had they attacked JMS of all places?

"We gotta save our boy!" Tay shouted.

He and Candace charged around me. Candace bulldozed through darkbringer after darkbringer like a bowling ball knocking down pins. Tay leaped over the carnage left behind her. Soon they turned the corner where the tentacle had disappeared with Winston in tow.

Nearby, three darkbringers had cornered a group of sixth graders who hadn't mastered their godling magic yet. "Not so fast," Frankie said as she sent balls of crackling energy that slammed the darkbringers into the lockers.

Eli had shimmered into a semi-invisible state down the hall. I could never get used to *seeing him* and *seeing through him* at the same time. "The OGs to the rescue!" he shouted.

"OGs?" one of the godlings near him asked.

"Original godlings," he announced proudly.

I knocked back the darkbringers who had surrounded me, but the one wearing a skull-and-bones T-shirt dodged my attack. He wasn't much taller than me, lanky, with hair shaved close to his scalp. His barbed tail whipped out and almost caught me across the cheek, but I ducked and jabbed the staff into his belly. That didn't stop him for long, though. He doubled over for a split second before his wings melted into writhing, black shadows that seared against my skin. I yelped in pain. "Time to die, guardian," the darkbringer snarled.

"Not today," I said through gritted teeth.

Real Talk: I was putting on a brave face, but I was scared. I swung my staff wildly, and it passed straight through the skull-and-bones boy's shadows. These darkbringers were much stronger than the ones we went up against last summer. How were we supposed to defeat them when most godlings were only just exploring their magic for the first time?

I concentrated all my energy on the staff, and the symbols grew brighter until several of them peeled off the wood and smacked the darkbringer square in the chest. That stopped him in his tracks. Literally. He fell flat on his back.

I barely had time to catch my breath as Frankie, Eli, and I ducked another attack. We fought back-to-back-to-back, just like old times. In the middle of the fight, I realized that Zeran was nowhere in sight. I glanced up and down the hallway, but he was gone. I tried to swallow my doubt as a darkbringer with three tails attempted to take off my head. I ducked, but one of the tails raked against my shoulder. RayShawn, a godling in eighth grade, sent a jet stream of water from the fountain, which hurtled the three-tailed darkbringer through the air.

"Thanks," I yelled, but I was still thinking about how

Zeran had disappeared as soon as we left the classroom.

"Where are the celestials?" Frankie lassoed two dark-bringers together with an energy rope. "We could really use some help."

She was right. Shangó, Ogun, and Principal Ollie pro-tected the school. If they weren't here, that meant more trouble.

"That's a perfectly reasonable question," I shouted.

Three dozen ghosts swept into the hallway, and Eli clapped his hands. "Ah, finally, my backup is here."

The ghosts advanced on the darkbringers, but a girl with bright-blue skin and white wings floated up from the floor. She had neon-pink hair that flowed around her shoul-ders. One by one, Eli's ghosts stopped. They were suddenly frozen in place like the rest of the humans. "They belong to me now," the girl said.

"Oh, heck naw." Eli cracked his knuckles. "Who do you think you are . . . snatching control of *my* army?"

"You must be the ghost boy I've heard so much about," the girl said, her voice low yet easily carrying over the chaos of the hall. "I am Carran, your self-proclaimed sworn enemy."

Eli grinned, looking proud of himself. "Too bad I've never heard of *you*."

Carran glared at him, her eyes blazing with fury. The ghosts grabbed godlings by their collars and jacked them up against lockers. "You have now," Carran spat.

"Help a fellow out, Eli," one of the ghosts begged in a paper-thin wisp of a voice.

"Are you going to let her show you up, man?" said another ghost.

"Come on, Eli," demanded a third. "Show this blue chick who's boss."

Eli scoffed with his fists on his hips, a trickle of sweat gliding down his forehead. "Well, Car-ran, you officially have an archnemesis." Blue magic swiveled around him and threaded through the ghosts' semitransparent forms. They suddenly went limp at that, and the godlings slipped out of their grasps.

"Nice try, E-li," Carran drawled. The ghosts all turned on him at once, their faces morphing into bloody eyes and sharp fangs. "I am the true master of the dead; you are only an amateur."

Eli took a step back. "Let's not be too hasty here."

"Leave him alone!" Frankie sent an energy ball at Carran, but the darkbringer didn't even blink. One of the ghosts leaped in front of her and absorbed the blow. Frankie was about to try again when Zeran snuck up behind her and twisted her arm behind her back.

"I've got this one," he called to Carran, then he pointed at me. "Take care of *her* and ghost boy."

My heart could've flown straight out of my chest,

but Zeran angled his face so Carran couldn't see him and winked. Was Zeran really on our side, or was he pretending? I shook the cobwebs out of my head. It didn't matter whether Zeran was a double or a triple agent right now. We had to stop Carran from controlling Eli's ghosts before she did some real damage.

Carran squinted at Zeran. "And who are you? You're not a part of my squadron."

"Of course not," Zeran said, jutting out his chin. "Your squadron couldn't get the job done, so our *lord* sent me. I'm part of an undercover unit."

Carran grimaced, her lips stretching over her teeth. "We don't need your help." She flipped her wrist. "Watch and learn."

Half of the ghosts who were advancing toward Eli turned their attention on me. Their skin was ghastly gray, and their fangs grew even longer. I had never seen Eli's ghosts like this before. Carran's magic had transformed them to the stuff of nightmares.

"This is not right on another level." Eli grimaced as we both backed away from the ghosts. "You can't just change *my* ghosts into some cartoon haunted-house version of themselves without regard for their feelings."

"'*Regard for their feelings*'?" Carran mocked him. "I don't care about the undead. They're only tools to do my bidding."

I shook my head. "The Lord of Shadows probably thinks the same thing about you."

Carran frowned, her forehead wrinkling as if she was considering what I said, but then she moaned, "Nice try, but I'm not a fool."

"Maybe we should agree on the definition of *fool* before you say that," I shot back, which only made Carran push the ghosts harder.

Blood trickled from Eli's nose, across his lip. The ghosts no longer begged him to stop Carran. She almost had complete control over them, but he was still trying to fight her.

Carran narrowed her eyes and tucked her chin against her chest. Her skin started to glow as the ghosts suddenly surged forward. With their teeth bared, they glided through the air at full speed. I ducked the first two that reached me, then I swept my staff up and through another ghost, who dispersed into gray smoke.

"How dare you dematerialize my ghosts!" Carran pouted.

"They're not you're ghosts," I said, turning two more into smoke. "Thief!"

While Carran's attention was on me, Zeran shrugged with a goofy smile on his face. He let Frankie go, and she launched another energy ball. This time Carran wasn't fast enough. The ball expanded into a net in midair and pinned her to the ceiling. She looked like a spider caught in a giant web. "You're going to regret that, you little pest," Carran screamed before I shot a green blob from my staff that landed across her mouth. She screamed against her muzzle.

"That's better," I said. "We're sick of hearing you babbling on with your nonsense."

"I seriously need a nap." Eli's eyelids fluttered closed. One by one, the ghosts around us faded. He leaned against the lockers, breathing hard. "I'm exhausted."

"I think they're retreating," Frankie cheered.

The darkbringers were losing ground. The godlings were holding their own. All those lessons with Ogun were finally paying off.

Down the hall, Winston appeared with blue flames dancing across his forearms. "You don't want none of this," he shouted at the darkbringers, his voice cocky. "I'm going to light you up."

I gulped. He meant that literally.

Candace was punching darkbringers clear across the room, and Tay sent shock waves through the floor to knock them down.

"Hey, Winston, looks like we're on the same side now," I called out as the last of the darkbringers fled. One of them had cut Carran out of Frankie's energy web, and she sulked as she ran with the others.

"Whatever, little Maya," Winston shot back.

I looked around at the godlings. They leaned against

lockers, cradling their injuries. They had bloodied noses, busted lips, cuts, and bruises. This was serious. Some slumped to the floor. From the looks of it, the darkbringers had been winning, so why did they retreat? It was almost like this had been a distraction.

"This isn't right," I said before a gateway opened in the middle of the hallway. Eleni ran out with another two dozen godlings on her trail before it snapped closed. Her voice came out in fits and starts as she doubled over with her hands on her knees.

"It's the celestials," Eleni said, gasping for breath. "They're in trouble."

ELEVEN

DID THOSE THINGS JUST MOVE?

I DOUBT THE ORISHAS are in trouble," Winston said as the flames on his skin extinguished. "They can handle these darkbringer clowns."

Zeran crossed his arms and glared at him. "I don't know what *clowns* are, but if it's coming from your mouth, it has to be an insult."

I rocked on my heels to calm my nerves. If the celestials were in trouble, then that meant we were in trouble too. "Where are they?"

Eleni's eyes filled with tears. "I saw them go into the library, then they disappeared."

Without another word, all of us—including Winston, Candace, and Tay—set off for the library. We rushed down the first-floor hallway and pivoted left into a second, much larger corridor. The library was at the very end with two arched double doors flanked by twin bronze mermaids. The one on the left was named Pearl, and the one on the right Diamond. According to JMS legend, they were servants of Mami Wata, a water spirit goddess.

Papa had told me that Mami Wata was a powerful celestial who opposed the rule about not interfering in human affairs. She and her servants had done their part to disrupt the slave trade that brought many people of African descent to the Americas. They'd made the sea treacherous and slipped onto ships at night to free as many people as they could. I didn't blame Mami Wata and the other celestials who stepped up, especially when said humans were using their powers to do bad things.

We skidded to a halt at the head of the corridor. Beyond the bronze mermaids, the library was pitch-black. Darkness bled across every bookshelf in sight, thrashing and twisting and hissing.

"What the heck is that?" Winston asked.

"Try to keep up, will you?" Eli said, grinning, but he looked nervous too. "Whatever that is, and I am not saying I know what it is, it's nothing compared to what we faced in the Dark."

"Are you sure about that, Eli?" Frankie mumbled under her breath. "Because that looks worse than the forest of hungry shadows and the flesh-eating grove."

"So you're saying that everything in the Dark wants to eat us?" Tay asked, his voice squeaky.

"Pretty much," Zeran answered with a smirk.

"No, thank you." Candace backed away. "I'm not going in there."

I shook my head. I'd expected Winston and his crew to duck out at the first chance. "We'll handle this."

"You'll handle this?" Winston laughed mockingly. "Quit playing, little Maya."

"Stop calling me *little*," I snapped. "My name is Maya. Call me that or don't talk to me."

"Dang, it was just a joke." Winston rolled his eyes. "Didn't know you were so sensitive . . ."

Zeran crossed his arms. "As if you really care."

"Fine, whatever," Winston moaned.

I tightened my grasp on the staff. "I'm going in."

"I'll go with you," Zeran said.

"You know I'm in," Frankie added.

Eleni was shaking as she stared into the darkness. She'd spent a thousand years stuck in a deep sleep while the Lord of Shadows used her magic to slowly destroy the veil between worlds. She had to be afraid that he'd try to do it again. "Are you okay?" I asked.

Her skin had faded to a shade paler, like she'd seen something far worse than a ghost. "The darkness . . . it's alive," she said. "I can feel it."

I bit my lip, trying to think of what to say to comfort her. When I saw her like this, it made me angry. I knew that she'd have to deal with her memories from the Dark her whole life. It wasn't like they would ever go away. The Lord of Shadows had to be stopped before he hurt more people. "You should stay here," I told her. "We can't risk walking into a trap. Someone needs to get help if we take too long to come back."

"I'll stay with you, Eleni," Eli said, looking a little better than he had after holding off Carran's attack. "I still can't call my ghosts. My powers are depleted."

"I'm going." Winston turned to Tay and Candace. "You two stay with ghost boy and the fairy girl."

"You really need to learn how to call people by their names." Eli shook his head. "It's the first step to *not* being a bully."

Winston stormed past us, acting like he had a clue what was going on, which was typical. Zeran groaned, and Frankie shrugged as we caught up with him halfway down the hall.

"Be careful, Maya," Eleni called after me.

"Always," I said, sounding more confident than I felt.

Frankie and Zeran flanked me while Winston led the way. The air grew colder the closer we got to the library entrance. A low hissing sound spilled from inside the library and made the hair on the back of my neck stand up. Trust me, that's really a thing that happens if you're scared enough.

As we reached the library entrance, the bronze mermaids opened their eyes and turned their glowing gazes on us. We stopped in our tracks, and Winston stumbled back. "Did those things just move?" he squeaked.

"The library is no longer safe for you, little ones," Pearl and Diamond said at the same time, their voices twins of each other—the same pitch, the same tone. It had the sound of a lullaby, and I had the strangest sensation of wanting to sleep. "Return to where it is safe."

"And they can talk, too?" Winston added in disbelief. "Quit playing."

I pushed back a yawn, fighting off the sudden sleepiness. "We have to go in there. Shangó, Ogun, and Principal Ollie are in trouble."

"You cannot help them," the mermaids lamented. "They are beyond this world."

Frankie wrapped an arm around her waist as if to ward off the news. "What does that mean?"

"Obviously it means they're dead," Winston barked at her. "Thought you were supposed to be so smart."

I couldn't accept that. No way. I'd seen the three celestials fight. They were strong. The darkbringers couldn't have gotten the best of them—not unless . . . I thought about Captain Nulan, how the Lord of Shadows had somehow gifted her a sliver of his magic. Had he done the same with other darkbringers? I swiped angrily at the tears rolling down my cheeks. "If it's all the same to you, we'd like to see for ourselves."

I stepped forward, and the mermaids' tails whipped from against the wall and formed a massive X across the entrance. The scales on their tails were made of teal and blue emeralds that pulsed against the gloom of the library beyond.

"Where are the other celestials?" Frankie asked. "Why haven't they come to help?"

"This is one of many attacks on the human world, and the others are tending to them," Pearl, the mermaid on the left, said. "Inside this library is a fracture between worlds that's far worse than a tear in the veil. Not even a guardian in training such as yourself, Maya, can repair it. Soon the wound will grow beyond our walls, but we will hold it back as long as we can with the help of the three celestials inside."

"Wait, they're still alive?" I asked. "Shangó, Ogun, and Principal Ollie?"

"They are in a state between life and death," Diamond answered after some consideration. "They are stopping the wound from spreading."

"Let us go inside," I insisted. "I might not be able to fix this wound, but we have to help the celestials."

"It is our job to protect the students of Jackson Middle School, not let them walk into danger," Pearl said, but she and her twin both looked conflicted about their choice.

"You said it already—it's only a matter of time before the wound breaks through your defenses," I said. "What happens when it does?"

"It will devour the school and continue to grow," Diamond answered as she reached up to wipe a single tear from her bronze cheek.

"More reason to let us try now," I said, tapping my foot impatiently.

The mermaids exchanged a glance before they turned back to us. "We sense great power and potential within you four children. Perhaps we should let you try, but it will pain us greatly if you do not return."

Winston smoothed his hand across his chin. "That power you feel is mostly me."

Ignoring him, I addressed Pearl and Diamond. "We know the risk."

The twins hesitated a moment longer before their tails whipped from in front of the door, clearing the way for us to enter. I stepped forward on shaky legs.

A fresh batch of blue flames lit across Winston's skin. "Are we sure about this?"

My staff glowed, encouraging me to be brave. "Sure as we're going to get."

"What Maya said," Frankie chimed in, electric currents crackling on her fingertips.

Two blue prods slipped from underneath Zeran's sleeves. "Yup."

I braced myself as we peered into the library. Inky blackness seeped between the two bronze mermaids. It was like looking into a vast nothingness with no beginning or end. Eli was wrong; this wasn't anything like what we'd faced in the Dark before. This was something much worse.

Twelve

Into the library we go

THE LIBRARY WAS alive with all the frightening and unexplainable sounds that in normal times—and let me tell you, these were far from *normal* times—could make for a good bedtime scary story. Cue the menacing hisses, low growls, devious cackles, et cetera, et cetera, et cetera. It was almost like the place was haunted, not that we were that lucky. Ghosts, we could handle. They were reasonable, *mostly*. I was willing to bet that whatever was in the library wouldn't listen to reason.

White particles floated out of the inky darkness, and Winston fanned his hand in front of his face. "Dust bunnies," he said, annoyed. "Really?"

Zeran dodged a swarm of them. "More like flesh-eating fleas."

"Fascinating," Frankie said. "I always thought those things were sentient."

"Only you would care," Winston groaned.

I got the feeling that fleas would be the least of our concerns. "Into the library we go," I mumbled. We had no time to waste.

As we stepped inside, Frankie's electric sparks, my staff, and Winston's blue flames illuminated a small pocket of space that pushed back the darkness. "Let's find the celestials and get out of here." Frankie said what we all must've been thinking. I didn't want to spend a minute longer here than we had to.

The library wasn't just the library anymore. Cold air whipped across our faces, and I could feel the hollowness of the space, like it was a large cavern. It was growing in size even now, moving and shifting, making room for *something*. It was almost as if a piece of the Dark itself had entered our world.

"This doesn't make sense," Winston said. "The library feels bigger."

"Under normal rules of science, maybe it doesn't make sense," Frankie said. "But like Maya once told me, magic explains the unexplainable. Listen to the sounds. Some are closer, while others are farther away. The library *is* bigger— much bigger."

Beyond the hissing and growls, I could hear whispering,

but I couldn't make out what the voices were saying. "We have a lot of ground to cover. I'll keep a lookout for what's in front of us. Frankie and Zeran, watch the flanks, and, Winston, you make sure nothing sneaks up behind us." Winston groaned under his breath, but he moved so he was behind me. I concentrated on the staff and sent down a plea. "Help us find the celestials."

Three symbols bathed in golden light peeled off the staff. Each symbol whispered the name of the celestial it represented: a hammer for Ogun, a lightning bolt for Shangó, and a feather for Principal Ollie. The symbols went three separate ways.

"Should we split up and follow them?" Zeran asked.

"No, I don't think so," I replied, getting a bad feeling. "We don't know what's in here with the celestials, and we have a better chance if we stay together. We can follow one symbol at a time."

"But which one first?" Frankie wondered aloud.

The others waited for me to pick. I'd seen all three of the celestial fight. They could hold their own. Principal Ollie single-handedly protected the seventh and eighth graders at the Field Museum when the Lord of Shadows sent his minions to possess Sue the Dinosaur. Ogun and Shangó had handled the darkbringer who could multiply himself while Papa was busy fixing a stubborn tear in the veil.

I looked at the golden symbols hovering a few feet away.

They each pulsed, but the feather, which represented Principal Ollie, pulsed the fastest. There was something frantic about it that reminded me of a racing heartbeat. Did that mean they were in the most trouble?

I bit my lip and made the call. "Principal Ollie."

No one questioned me as we set off to follow the feather. We kept pushing back vines that crawled across our feet and ankles and shadows that hissed at the edges of our vision like venomous snakes. Another howl rang out. One that was very close—*too* close.

Winston's eyes went wide. "Was that General?"

General was always with Ogun, so he had to be in the library too.

"That sounds like a Tazar," Zeran said, looking around with his prods ready.

"A what?" Winston asked. It wasn't my imagination that his voice had gone hoarse.

Zeran thought a moment, then he answered, "It's like a really big dog."

"That's an understatement," I said as we moved deeper into the library. General was a really big dog. Tazars were huge. Instead of fur, scales covered their bodies, and they had a row of sharp spikes across their backs. Frankie, Eli, and I had almost run into them when we were searching for my father's soul.

If the library was a wound between our world and

the Dark, then anything—*or anyone*—could cross over. It reminded me of a gaping sore that oozed pus. Gross, I know, but it was the most accurate way to describe it. The other celestials were powerful, but only a guardian had the magic to fix the veil. Maybe I could heal this, too. I had to try, even if Pearl and Diamond didn't think I could.

I imagined the wound knitting back together, stitch by stitch. My magic poured out of me, through the staff, so much of it that my skin turned hot. I quickly realized that there was no focal point like a regular tear, nothing to latch on to. Sweat streaked down my cheeks. It wasn't working. I could still sense the library expanding, which meant that the wound was growing. "Ugh," I said, giving up.

"Squawk" came a high-pitched cry right before an impundulu sauntered into our path. We stopped in our tracks. Okay, so I should have seen the giant-killer-bird angle coming. The impundulu shrieked again as it stretched out its rainbow-colored wings and reared back. The needle-sharp spines on its underbelly stood up.

"I got this one," Winston said as he raised his hands and shot flames at the impundulu.

"Don't!" I nudged him with the staff, deflecting his aim. His fire went over the bird's head.

Winston shoved the staff away. "Why did you do that?"

The impundulu shrieked once more, and the second time it sounded more desperate. A baby impundulu shuffled from behind the bird with tiny iridescent wings. It was so young that it hadn't grown its spines yet. "Impundulu only attack to protect their young. If we leave it be, it'll go away."

When the impundulu and its chick disappeared into the shadows, Winston said, "When that thing comes back to pluck out your eyes, don't ask for my help."

I let out a sharp laugh. "Like I would ever ask you for anything."

Frankie pointed. "Principal Ollie's symbol stopped."

We ran to catch up with the symbol. It landed on something suspended in the air. The moment we got closer, we all gasped. It was Principal Ollie, but they'd turned translucent, like they were fading in and out between worlds.

"What are you kids doing here?" they asked, hovering above us.

"Um . . . we came to rescue you," I said, but it sounded like a question.

Principal Ollie shifted back into their physical form. They wore a dark gray suit, a crisp white shirt, a neon-blue tie, and shiny leopard-print shoes. Leave it to them to still look so put together in the middle of a battle. "There's nothing you can do here," they said. "Shangó, Ogun, and I will keep the wound from spreading as long as we can."

"But . . ." I started.

"No *buts*, Miss Abeola," Principal Ollie snapped. "Tell Yemoja . . ."

Before they could finish speaking, shadows shot out and lashed around them. It happened so quickly that we were caught off guard for a split second. *Oh, heck naw.* I swung my staff, and glowing god symbols careened at the shadows, but the symbols turned to ashes. Winston sent flames that fizzled out on impact. Zeran hit them with the prods. Frankie tried her electric current, but the shadows completely enveloped the celestial.

"What . . . what is even happening?" Winston stuttered. "The shadows . . . they're trying to eat Principal Ollie."

"We've been telling you all along this isn't a game," I shouted at him. Maybe I shouldn't have taken out my frustration on Winston, but this wasn't the time for him to be just figuring out the basics.

Principal Ollie's light began to pulse until it pushed back the shadows, which hissed and shrieked as they retreated. "This is the only way to slow him down," Principal Ollie said, voice weak. "Tell Yemoja that it's too late."

Him—*him.* H-I-M. There was only one *him.* The creepy stuff of nightmares that made boogeymen look like cream puffs. A man who was dead set on destroying everyone and everything in the human world. Not a man. A celestial with unthinkable power. The Lord of Shadows.

"Is he here?" I asked desperately. "Is the Lord of Shadows here?"

But Principal Ollie had fallen eerily still, leaving my

question unanswered. They became pure light, bright and beautiful.

"I think they're in some kind of stasis," Frankie suggested. "The mermaids said that the celestials were using their powers to keep the wound from spreading. There's nothing we can do."

"What about Ogun and Shangó?" Zeran said. "Should we look for them?"

Before anyone could answer, a burst of familiar cackling came from behind us. Four pairs of glowing yellow eyes stared at us from the shadows. Frankie and I looked at each other in horror, remembering the night we'd gotten cornered in an alley. "Werehyenas," we said at the same time.

Zeran frowned. "*Were* . . . what?"

"You have to be kidding me," Winston said as the werehyenas stepped into the light. Standing on their hind legs, they were nearly seven feet tall, their ears sticking up. Their lips were pulled back, revealing very sharp teeth.

"I wonder how they got into the library," Frankie said, shrinking back.

I grimaced as we faced the werehyenas, who looked mighty hungry. "I think that's beside the point."

Winston shot flames at the lead werehyena, but they turned into puffs of smoke as soon as they hit the alpha's spotted fur. "Oh, snap!"

I was beginning to think that his solution to every

problem was to attempt to set it on fire.

"We've stumbled upon a tasty snack," snarled the alpha. He was bigger and meaner looking than the other three. "A morsel for each of us."

The werehyenas pounced and we scattered, dodging the attack. The alpha bounced off an invisible shield around Principal Ollie, did a backflip, and landed on its feet. Under any other circumstances, that might have been impressive, but not when four massive furballs were trying to eat you. They stalked toward us, drool dripping from their mouths.

"Time to die, *little morsels*," snarled the alpha. "I've always wanted to eat a godling and taste their magic."

Zeran and I stood back-to-back. "I'm not a godling," he moaned.

"And I really resent being called a morsel," Winston grumbled.

There was something vaguely satisfying in seeing something finally make Winston sweat. It served him right for always making fun of me and the other kids at JMS.

"These werehyenas are not half as scary as they pretend to be," I said defiantly.

"I'm not so sure about that," Frankie chimed in.

Just then, a loud growl echoed from the shadows. I held my breath until General—Ogun's bloodhound—stepped forward with all six of his eyes focused on the werehyenas. Two pairs were on the alpha. General was a big dog, but he was half the size of the werehyenas, who quickly dropped to all fours to face him. General didn't tuck his tail and run. Instead, he bared a mouth full of razor-sharp teeth.

I gulped. "This is about to get ugly."

General leaped at the werehyenas. Soon the five of them were a tangle of fur and swiping claws. The alpha went for General's neck, but the bloodhound threw his weight into the werehyena. General was fast, though not fast enough. The alpha's teeth sank into his shoulder. General yelped in pain. We had to help him. I raised my staff, but just as I was about to let off a shot, the shadows closed around them and cut off all sounds of their fight.

"I told you that I would see you again soon, Maya" came a voice as smooth as silk, a voice that sent a chill through my whole body. For a moment, I couldn't move, couldn't breathe. He couldn't be here. *Couldn't be.* But no amount of denying it would change the truth. I wasn't dreaming, nor was I on the crossroads. This was real.

I slowly turned around, my back and legs stiff. The Lord of Shadows peered at me with glowing violet eyes before he let out a hoarse laugh that set ice in my veins and almost brought me to my knees.

THIRTEEN

TIME TO GO

I STOOD OPPOSITE THE Lord of Shadows, my heart racing, my palms sweating. My stomach felt as if I had swallowed a bag of rocks. I was rooted in place, frozen with fear. Had I really thought this day wouldn't come—that he wouldn't find a way through the veil? I had to pull myself together. This wasn't over yet, not by a long shot. In fact, it had just begun. The light from my staff illuminated the bulk of the Lord of Shadows, but he wasn't as I remembered. He was in some kind of husk with a cocoon of blackness swirling around him.

I shook my head in disbelief. "You can't be here."

"I wouldn't have made it this far without your help," the Lord of Shadows said, his voice laced with amusement. He was mocking me. "It's ironic. The daughters of my eternal enemy are the key to destroying the veil."

I swallowed hard and pushed back my tears. This moment was surreal, like waking up from a bad dream to find out that reality was even worse. I tried to hold on to what Papa told me this morning. Adults like the Lord of Shadows didn't want to take responsibility for their own bad behavior. I understood it, yet I still felt angry that he used my magic to create the wound in the veil.

"So, you're the Lord of Shadows?" Winston's mouth curled into a grimace. "You don't look so tough to me." He stepped closer, flame licking his hands. "I'm going to end this now."

"Winston, don't," Frankie shouted, but it was too late.

The Lord of Shadows' purple and black ribbons whipped out and latched around Winston's wrists. He let out a blood-curdling scream and dropped to his knees. His knuckles turned ash gray, then his face, his hair. Even though he was the biggest bully I knew, I sprang into action. No one deserved this fate. Not even him.

I swung my staff at the ribbons, and Frankie let loose two energy balls. Zeran attacked with his prod. But Winston had gone completely still as the ribbons dragged him toward the Lord of Shadows.

"It isn't working!" Frankie shouted.

I ducked a shadow that snapped at my face. "We have to keep trying."

Suddenly a warm light pulsed above our heads, and

I shielded my eyes as I looked up. It was vaguely human shaped with the impression of double axes across its back. It had to be Ogun, the god of war, or what was left of him. The library began to shake, and a biography of Jean Baptiste Point du Sable, the father of Chicago, flew across the room, heading straight for the Lord of Shadows. Glowing god symbols flew from the pages of the book in a wild flurry. Hundreds of them, thousands. They sliced into the Lord of Shadows and shredded his cocoon. It was enough of a distraction that his ribbons dropped Winston and formed a wall of darkness to protect him.

"Take that!" Frankie cheered, pumping her fist in the air. "Courtesy of the celestials."

The Lord of Shadows glared at her, his violet-colored eyes narrowing. If looks could kill, we would be goners by now. The du Sable biography lay on the floor in front of the Lord of Shadows, the last god symbols fading to dust. "Do you think tricks will stop me? Are you really so naive?" He slipped another smile on his face. This one was more devious than the last. "Your mother, Zala, was naive too, so I've been told."

Frankie froze at that, her eyes wide. Her lips trembled as she demanded, "Did you send those Azurians after my mom?"

I wouldn't put it past the Lord of Shadows to see her as a threat. He was relentless and would do anything to get what he wanted.

"No," he said without any emotion. "She never got in my way."

Frankie balled her hands into fists as electricity flickered across her knuckles. The Lord of Shadows' answer seemed only to make her angrier. "Well, *I'm* in your way." She drew herself up to her full height. "We all are."

"Foolish children," the Lord of Shadows said as he sank deeper into his cocoon.

For all his boasting about destroying the veil, he was still weak, or else he would've pounced on us already. "You're stuck here, aren't you?" I gestured at the library. "The celestials have you trapped."

"For now." Flakes of black ash fell from his face, revealing iridescent skin the color of the moon. "Soon, I will be free, and when I am, I will exact my revenge against your precious celestials. I will destroy everything they cherish and give this world back to the darkbringers and the magical creatures forced to live in the shadows. Say goodbye to your families while you still can."

This wasn't the first time the Lord of Shadows had threatened our families, but it was the first time he'd done it with one foot already in the human world. I couldn't believe that he was trying to justify his actions. He didn't care about the darkbringers or anyone else for that matter. If he had, he wouldn't have been bent on starting a war. I gripped my staff so hard that my fingers ached. "I won't let you hurt anyone else."

He laughed, then his next words sent icicles down my spine. "You can't stop me."

I lurched forward, but Zeran grabbed my arm. "We're not going to win this one."

He was right. The darkness pushed against Ogun's light. It was growing, ballooning out like storm clouds. Winston moaned as he tried and failed to get to his feet. His skin was still gray, but his color was slowly coming back. Zeran helped him up.

I backed away from the Lord of Shadows, my pulse throbbing. We couldn't let him enter our world, but was it already too late? His words echoed in my mind: *for now.*

A howl rose from the shadows, and I snapped my head around just in time to see General trotting toward us. I was glad that he was okay after going up against the were-hyenas, though he was bleeding from several bites and scratches. He stopped at my side and nudged me with his massive head—*time to go.* We ran, with General leading the way.

When we reached the library entrance, I glanced over my shoulder. Three bright lights hovered in the air. I blinked back tears. Principal Ollie, Shangó, and Ogun had become pure energy, and still, the shadows were climbing inch by inch. They crawled up the bookshelves and the walls like oily, black snakes.

This was an absolute disaster, and it was partly my fault.

If I hadn't let the Lord of Shadows trick me into touching the amplifier, he wouldn't have been able to damage the veil this much. I had to fix this. I knew I couldn't do it alone, but there had to be a way. We might have retreated for now, but I wouldn't give up.

By the time we passed beneath the mermaid guardians, I was out of breath. A whooshing sound filled my ears, and the dizziness hit me at once. I found the nearest wall to lean against and squeezed my eyes closed. My lungs ached.

Eleni was at my side in an instant, hovering like a mother hen, but I didn't mind it. When I first found out that Papa had another family before Mama and me, I didn't know how I felt about it. Even when Eleni came to live with us, I wasn't sure we'd get along, but now I couldn't imagine my life without her. "I shouldn't have let you go," she said. "I'm the oldest. It's my job to protect you. I shouldn't have been so scared."

When I opened my eyes, Eleni squeezed me in a bear hug. "There's nothing wrong with being afraid," I told her. "As guardians of the veil, we have to face some scary stuff, but we'll always have each other's back, okay?"

Eleni sniffled as she pulled away. "You promise?"

"I promise," I said.

General whined and rubbed his cold nose against my leg. He looked up at me with his three pairs of sad eyes. The mermaids had erected a solid wall in front of the entrance, as if the library had never had doors. The sign above the mermaids carved into the stone had changed.

"'*The dark eve is nearly upon us,*'" Eleni said, reading the new inscription.

"Well, that's not ominous at all," Eli mumbled under his breath.

Zeran, Frankie, and I filled Eleni and him in on what happened in the library. Eleni scratched General's neck, and he sat on his haunches. "It'll be okay, boy," she said, but she didn't sound all that convinced.

More godlings poured into the hall. Winston had gotten most of his color back, and Candace and Tay were fussing over him. "The Lord of Shadows better be glad Zeran pulled me out," he told his friends, clearly enjoying the attention. "If not, I would have defeated him on the spot."

"Is he always this full of himself?" Zeran asked, leaning against the wall beside Eleni.

"Yes," Frankie and I both answered.

Eli crossed his arms. "Forget about Winston. I want to know how the heck the Lord of Shadows is so much more powerful than the celestials. I don't get it."

"The Lord of Shadows *is* a celestial," Zeran reminded him.

"And he was the universe's first child," Eleni said, still staring blankly at the stone wall in front of the library. "He was born many millennia before the other celestials. Thus, he has been drawing strength from the universe for much longer."

I frowned, my head spinning. A half-formed idea danced around the edges of my mind. No one was invincible, not even a celestial. What was his kryptonite . . . his Achilles' heel? "So how do we break his connection to the universe?"

"I don't think we can disconnect him from the universe," Frankie said, taking her glasses off. She used her shirttail to clean the lens. "Everything is contained inside the universe. Technically there is no *outside*—like that actually defies logic."

"Drop him in a black hole," Gail Galanis suggested. She had wandered over from the group surrounding Winston. "My cousin did that to a lava-spitting monster that attacked the island of Crete."

My friends gawked at Gail in disbelief until she told them that her great-great-great-great-grandmother was a Titan, though no one in her family could say which one.

Eli arched one eyebrow. "So you're a godling . . . Wait, no, a demigod?"

"Not exactly." Gail grimaced. "But I am immune to the effects of most magic."

"Godlings!" said Oshun sharply. She'd suddenly appeared in the hallway in a halo of mist. "Return to your classrooms."

Nana materialized beside her, and the two celestials swept toward the library. None of the godlings left—we watched Nana press her hands against the slab of stone blocking the library.

"Ollie, Ogun, and Shangó are inside," Nana said, voice hollow. "They're alive."

Oshun let out a sigh of relief. "Thank the heavens."

Nana frowned with her hand still pressed against the stone. "He . . . *the Lord of Shadows* is almost through the veil."

"He dares break through in our sanctuary—*a place of peace*!" Oshun hissed.

Oshun was missing the bigger point. The Lord of Shadows had broken into the sanctuary because he could. It was his way of showing the celestials that they couldn't stop him from entering the human world, not even when it was right under their noses.

"We have to reinforce the barrier," Nana said, resigned.

"But . . . what about my brothers and Ollie?" Oshun asked. "We can't just leave them."

"No choice." Nana shook her head. "They've bought us time."

Oshun nodded reluctantly and pressed her hand next to Nana's. Magic rippled across the stone slab in waves. The guardian mermaids' iridescent tails shimmered as if they were absorbing the celestials' power.

"But how long will that last?" Eli whispered next to me.

"Not long, I'm willing to bet," I said quietly.

When the celestials were done reinforcing the barrier, Oshun shouted, losing her patience, "Get back to your classrooms now, *godlings*!"

I crossed my arms, still shaking from our encounter with the Lord of Shadows. Some of the other godlings started to file out of the hallway, but I wasn't going to let Oshun intimidate me into leaving. I was a guardian, and any breaks through the veil were my territory. The rest of my friends stayed, too. "Where were you and the rest of the celestials? Maybe we could've stopped him."

Oshun turned her cutting smile on me. "To answer your question, young guardian, we came as soon as we were done helping Elegguá. The Lord of Shadows almost broke through the veil in several places all at once, which wouldn't have happened if you hadn't convinced Yemoja not to destroy the Dark world."

I was speechless. My friends were staring at me, and so were the few other godlings who were taking their sweet time leaving.

"The Lord of Shadows can do that?" Gail's eyebrows shot up. "That would be cool if it were anyone else, I guess."

Oshun frowned at Gail, looking puzzled.

"Not a godling," Gail moaned.

"I can see that," Oshun said. "Go to your classroom."

"It sucks to always be on the sidelines." Gail sighed, then stalked off.

"I'd gladly let you take my place," Eli called after her. "Except I get to keep my ghosts."

"Yeah, yeah," she said before disappearing around a corner.

Nana looked up at the guardian mermaids, Pearl and Diamond, who were both shimmering with light all over now. "Yemoja would have waited for the others to arrive before attempting to destroy the Dark either way, and there was no guarantee that it would have worked. We always knew this day would come—it was inevitable. We couldn't hold him back forever."

"But we *had* a chance." Oshun blinked back tears. "Now we don't."

I was numb inside, stunned by the news. Still, I couldn't justify Yemoja and the other celestials destroying an entire world to rid themselves of the Lord of Shadows. But now the decision to wait had put all of us in grave danger. The Lord of Shadows had one foot in our world already, and it wouldn't be long before he completely crossed the veil.

FOURTEEN

WE'RE DOOMED

NEAR THE END of first period, I was so over it. I couldn't concentrate. The Lord of Shadows was in the library, protected in a cocoon, and the Dark was bleeding across the books and periodicals. With the other wounds in the veil closed, Papa and the rest of the celestials had returned. Yemoja had glamoured the whole east wing of the school so no one—godling or human—could enter it by accident. With their magic, they'd whipped up a replica of the library, teachers' lounge, and classrooms. But I knew the truth, and so did the other godlings: the celestials' greatest, most dangerous enemy was only a few steps away.

I watched the clock and counted down the minutes. I hated waiting around to see what would happen next. Most of the godlings were sneaking their hands under their tables and glancing down at their phones. All anyone could talk about were the darkbringers and the Lord of Shadows. I was surprised that school wasn't canceled yet, but then again, it sounded like the Lord of Shadows was contained for now. That didn't make me any less jumpy.

Our English teacher, Ms. Taylor, had her back to the classroom as she drew a graphical representation of the parts of a story. She and the human kids were completely oblivious to the chatter, which had to be the celestials' doing. "The events leading up to the conclusion of the story represent the rising action. Think of it as the calm before the storm. It should be full of tension and anticipation."

"My brother says another celestial arrived today," Naomi Reynolds blurted out, swiping her finger across her phone screen. "He wasn't sure which one, but he says the celestial was ten feet tall. He came right before the Lord of Shadows ripped a hole in the library."

Maurice Miller, who always slept in class, raised his head from his desk and yawned. "It doesn't matter who comes. We're doomed, and the celestials are too stubborn to admit it."

"If you keep talking like that, we might as well be." I added my two cents.

"Why haven't the celestials canceled classes already?" Tay grumbled. "I want to be far away from that maniac."

Candace leaned forward with her elbows propped

on her table. "If Principal Ollie were here, they would've already sent us home by now."

"We're not going to let the Lord of Shadows run us out of JMS." Winston crossed his arms. "If he wants a fight, he'll get one."

For once, I agreed with Winston. I didn't want the celestials to shut down the school. But knowing them, they hadn't decided what to do yet. They always took so long to deliberate on their decisions, but sometimes you needed to act quickly. "We'll find a way to stop him."

"This is your fault, Maya," Winston snapped. "The Lord of Shadows and his darkbringers would be dust right now if not for you."

Everyone was staring at me again. I wanted to crawl under my desk and hide, but I wasn't going to let Winston or anyone else make me feel ashamed for wanting to do the right thing.

"We all heard what Oshun said," Tisha Thomas butted in. "You convinced the celestials not to destroy the Dark."

"None of you have even been to the Dark," I shot back. "It's not a mythological place, okay? There are people there . . . people like Zeran." I looked at him, and he'd gone stone-faced. I couldn't believe that we were even discussing this. "We're not mass murderers, you know?"

"We aren't, but from what I hear, your dad is," Winston mumbled under his breath. "Also, I heard what the

Lord of Shadows said. You helped him destroy the veil. You whole family is bad news."

I jumped out of my seat, fuming, and Zeran and Frankie both held me back. Winston—the biggest bully at JMS—had some nerve calling my family bad news. "Say that to my face."

Winston smirked. "I just did."

"He's not worth it," Zeran said through gritted teeth.

Ms. Taylor turned around from the chalkboard, her eyes slightly out of focus. "Did you have a question, Maya? Why are you out of your seat?"

I shook my head in disbelief. Ms. Taylor and the human kids had the right to know what was happening right under their noses; instead, they were walking around in a daze induced by magic. "No, ma'am," I said, glaring at Winston. Everyone knew that Papa had made a mistake with the veil, but he wasn't the only celestial who'd made mistakes. No one was perfect, but it was really bad when an immortal messed up. And the Lord of Shadows using my and Eleni's magic to damage the veil? That was on him—not me.

After the bell rang, Frankie, Zeran, and I rushed out of Ms. Taylor's classroom, glad to be free of Winston, if only for a few minutes between classes. The hallway was swarming with older godlings. The ice cream truck driver, who everyone called Big Boy; Calvin from the barbershop; Jerome, who ran the food bank; Rhonda, Leroy, and Carla from the community center. Two cashiers from the grocery store, the sensei from the dojo, and a dozen others. They wore matching uniforms of all black with gold diagonal stripes across the chest.

"What are they doing?" Zeran asked as they passed by us.

"Maybe they're here to help the celestials," Frankie said.

If the celestials couldn't stop the Lord of Shadows, what chance did these godlings have? Better yet, what chance did *we* have? I tried to push the thought out of my mind as Eli caught up with us. Zeran headed off to math, which he had with Gail, Tisha, and Candace, while the rest of us set off for science.

When Frankie, Eli, and I stepped into the lab, we looked longingly at the empty desk in front of the room. Mr. Jenkins, aka Shangó, had formulas scribbled across the board.

Frankie blinked at the whiteboard. "Interesting."

"What's interesting?" Eli arched one eyebrow. "Paranormal-level interesting or *normal-likely-boring* interesting?"

"It looks like Shangó, um, I mean Mr. Jenkins, was working on a theory about dark energy," Frankie said as we climbed into our chairs. When Eli and I both cocked our heads, she explained. "Dark energy makes up about sixty-eight percent of the universe, but scientists don't know why the energy exists, only that this dark energy causes the universe to expand faster and faster. Meaning that the universe is growing at an accelerated rate."

I crossed my arms on our table and put my head down. I did not care about a theory on dark energy. Studying space right now was the last thing on my mind. It just seemed so irrelevant and a little disrespectful to talk about when we knew that Shangó, Ogun, and Principal Ollie were in trouble.

"According to these equations, he thought that dark energy could be recalibrated to create a vacuum in space," Frankie continued.

"Will you give it a rest?" Winston yelled from across the room. "Shangó isn't here for you to impress with your nerdiness. You're just making stuff up anyway. You don't understand those equations."

"I understand them more than you do," Frankie countered.

"That's enough" came a cranky voice that I would know anywhere. Miss Ida Johnston stepped into our class juggling a stack of science books. "We will not speculate on theories."

I groaned as I lifted my head. Of the cranky Johnston twins, by far, Miss Ida was the crankier one. She was wearing a plain, shapeless gray dress that was one shade darker than her gray hair, which she had in a puffy bun. "Are you our substitute teacher?" I resisted adding, *What's even the point?*

Miss Ida placed her books on Shangó's desk. "Don't look so overjoyed to see me, Miss Abeola."

Well, that was a first, her calling me Miss Abeola. I sat up straight in my chair.

"For those who don't know me, I will be stepping in for *Mr. Jenkins* today," she said to the class. "You may call me Miss Johnston. My twin sister will be fulfilling Principal Ollie's duties. You may call her Miss Johnston too."

"How are we going to tell you apart?" someone asked.

"With your eyes," Miss Ida said, glaring at the kid.

"What happened to Mr. Jenkins and Principal Ollie?" asked a human student. "I saw them both this morning."

"They, along with *Zane*, your crossing guard, are away doing important work," she explained.

"What important work?" asked another kid.

"Enough questions!" Miss Ida said as she turned to the whiteboard and erased Shangó's theories on dark energy. "Today's lesson will be a refresher on cells and cell structure."

"What makes her qualified to teach science?" Winston whispered to Tay.

"For your information, I hold twelve separate advanced degrees, three of which are relevant to this class. Any further outbursts will result in extra homework for the winter break and detention for a month."

That's if the Lord of Shadows doesn't destroy our world by then, I thought.

Winston groaned, but he kept his mouth shut for the rest of the period. I couldn't say I was paying attention, nor were any of the godlings. We all looked dejected. Sure, the school nurse had healed any visible injuries from the battle, but not all injuries could be seen. We were hurting, licking our wounds. The Lord of Shadows had made his move, and we were caught unprepared.

Miss Ida was halfway through her lesson when the school intercom sparked to life with Miss Lucille's voice. "Hello, JMS students! Today there will be a special assembly in the gym at noon. Bag lunches will be provided, and school will let out shortly after that due to an . . . *infestation* in the library. Your families have been made aware, and we have arranged for everyone to get home safely."

"*Infestation*," one of the godlings blurted out. "That's putting it lightly."

"We're getting out early!" a human kid cheered. "Sweet!"

Frankie and Eli exchanged nervous glances. I was worried, too. The assembly had to be about our current predicament with the Lord of Shadows. Maybe I was wrong about the celestials taking forever to make a decision on anything.

After science class, we met up with Zeran and Eleni as we all filed out of the main building and trekked to the gym for the assembly. The mood was solemn—even the human kids had caught on that something was wrong.

A line formed in front of the gym. I didn't realize it at first, but whenever a human student or teacher entered the double doors, there was a barely visible glimmer.

"Where are the other students going?" I asked an older godling in a black-and-gold uniform.

"The humans will be attending a *different* assembly," the godling answered.

Inside were all the godlings from the elementary school, the high school, and all across the neighborhood alongside JMS students. The gym was buzzing with gossip as we found space on the bleachers.

"No way they're coming back. Mom said the Lord of Shadows is too powerful."

"Winston almost beat the Lord of Shadows, so there's a chance."

"Did you see Winston when they pulled him out of the library? He was toast."

"How can we hope to stand against an entire army of dark-bringers?"

Eleni leaned against my shoulder, and I wrapped my arm around her. Frankie was on my opposite side, and Eli and Zeran sat on the row above us. After everyone had settled on the bleachers, Yemoja and the other celestials glided to the middle of the basketball court. Her sea-green dress moved like calming ocean waves. It was hypnotizing. Papa, Nana, Eshu, and three celestials I hadn't met before stood behind her.

"The really tall one is Orunmila, one of the universe's first children," I heard someone whisper. "He is the orisha of wisdom, knowledge, and divination . . ."

Yemoja cleared her throat, and everyone fell silent as if in a trance. "By now, you know that Principal Ollie and my children, Ogun and Shangó, have given themselves over to stop the Lord of Shadows from entering our world." Her voice was a song on the wind that washed over the gym— calm and soothing, even though inside I felt raging fire. "It will not be enough, but for now, it has trapped the essence of him in one place. He will not be able to break through the veil elsewhere."

She looked over the crowd, blinking back tears. "As we speak, I am arranging for your human neighbors to be relocated. The neighborhood will be completely isolated and shielded in our final attempt to contain the Lord of Shadows."

Frankie nervously bounced her foot. She was shaking. We all were. I thought of the dream I had at the beginning of the summer. The Lord of Shadows had stood at the end of my block. His hundreds of purple and black ribbons lashed out around him, writhing and leeching the color from everything. The trees had turned gray, along with the cars, the stop sign, the grass, the houses. He had relished draining the life out of our neighborhood.

Mama always said that some people couldn't be reasoned with—that no matter how sound the argument, how clear the facts, some people were so consumed with their own hatred that they would never find a middle ground or do what was best for everyone. I did not doubt that the Lord of Shadows was one of those people, but some part of me wanted to try just once to reason with him. No one else had to die because of past mistakes.

"We are much weakened after our last battle against the Lord of Shadows," Yemoja continued, studying the faces in the crowd. "We can't defend this world alone. We need your help, but I will not lie to you. Some of you will not survive."

"How did the Lord of Shadows break through at the school?" someone asked.

"Maybe he had help from the darkbringer," said another.

People stared and pointed at Zeran, but he didn't shrink in his seat. "Why would I still be here if I betrayed you? Make it make sense, because right now you're just scared."

"He's not the one you should be worried about," I said, though I hadn't forgotten that he'd disappeared when the darkbringers first attacked. "He's on our side."

"Says the girl who befriended him and brought him back from the Dark," Tisha Thomas shouted from the other end of the bleachers. "Who's to say that we can even trust him? I, for one, don't." Whispers rose in the crowd, many agreeing with her.

"I trust him!" Eli jumped to his feet. "Zeran saved our lives more than once. He went up against the Lord of Shadows, Tyana Nulan, and his own father to help us. None of you have the right to doubt him without any evidence."

Most people had the sense to look ashamed, but others like Tisha Thomas wouldn't back down. She believed the future she saw of Zeran betraying me, and I had to consider it. Maybe if he weren't always finding excuses to go off by himself, I wouldn't still have doubts.

"Perhaps there are other darkbringers like Zeran who would stand against the Lord of Shadows," Nana said, "but I would be surprised if there are more than a few."

"Excuse me for saying this, but you have no idea what you're talking about," Zeran said. "You know nothing about my people—none of you do—only what you think you know, which clearly isn't much."

Nana cocked an eyebrow. No one talked to her like that unless they were prepared for a tongue-lashing.

"Whether or not the darkbringers are willing to help is beside the point right now." Papa spoke up. I could hear the pain in his voice, the way his words cracked around the edges. "Zeran has shown true loyalty to my daughter and her friends. We would be no better than the Lord of Shadows if we condemned him over the actions of a few. Our mistake is perhaps failing to find a way to reason with the Lord of Shadows, instead of confining him to the Dark world to start with. A moment ago, someone asked how he broke through the veil. I'm afraid the answer is simple: the veil has weakened beyond repair."

People stared at Papa with wide eyes, some mumbling, some stunned.

Yemoja raised a hand to silence the crowd. "We'll begin evacuating the younger godlings and their human families to Azur immediately. By the time you go home to pack your things, there will be a note waiting for you with your scheduled departure time."

"What's going to happen to the rest of the humans?" someone asked.

"We're working on a plan for them," Yemoja said, assuring him.

"What does that even mean?" I whispered under my breath.

Papa looked to Eleni and me, his face filled with guilt. Eleni let out a small gasp. I should've known as soon as Yemoja said that some celestials would stay behind in the neighborhood. I shook my head, refusing to accept it.

Papa couldn't leave Mama, Eleni, and me. Nor could he expect us to go to Azur without him. If he was staying behind to fight the Lord of Shadows, then so was I. I couldn't stop being a guardian in training just because things got hard. If anything, now was the time to bring my A game.

FIFTEEN

I MEET MY MATCH

WHEN YEMOJA DISMISSED the assembly, most of the godlings filed out of the gym in a somber mood, leaving only the JMS students. The older godlings had volunteered to fight, but Yemoja had said that no one under seventeen would be allowed to join the battle. That was completely unfair.

I stepped off the bleachers, intending to protest. I was a guardian, and if any godling got to stay behind, it should be me. Eleni and I accidentally helped damage the veil, but maybe there was a way to repair it if we worked together. We couldn't do that if we were hiding on Azur.

"There isn't much time," Yemoja was telling the other orishas. They spoke in hushed voices. "We'll set up three perimeters around the Lord of Shadows with celestials and godlings in each group. Sky Father and I will lead the first line of defense around the library. Nana, your group will secure the school grounds. Finally, Elegguá, you will create a seal around the neighborhood." Yemoja paused, and for a moment, the sound of crashing waves filled my ears, like a storm on a sea.

Papa's eyes were red rimmed, and he looked so tired. "The seal won't hold him long. He's much stronger than when we faced him in the last war."

Yemoja clasped his shoulder affectionally. "I don't see that we have another choice, old friend. Once the seal is intact, it will be our last line of defense. It should be enough to delay the Lord of Shadows while we evacuate this world."

"Since we cannot defeat him with sheer might, we must outwit him," Orunmila said, his voice quiet. He was tall with dark skin and a disc of light glowing around his head.

"In case you've forgotten, we haven't been able to outwit him either," Nana said.

I thought about Shangó's dark energy equations. At first, I had dismissed them as just another science problem to solve, but maybe he was working on a way to defeat the Lord of Shadows. I turned back to the bleachers, where my friends were having their own conversation.

Eli squinted. "Is it just me, or do the celestials look *real* nervous over there?"

"They're not the only ones," Frankie said. "We're all nervous."

"You should be," Zeran chimed in. He sat with his back straight as a board. "I'm afraid of what the Lord of Shadows will do to your world."

He'll destroy it. I didn't say my thought out loud. I wasn't superstitious, but why test fate? "Frankie," I said, changing the subject. Enough of this doom and gloom. We needed answers. "Do you think that Shangó was right, that dark energy could be used to create a vacuum in space?"

"I don't see how it's implausible." Frankie shrugged. "But then again, I thought magic was implausible until last summer." She rubbed her chin. "If like Eleni said, the Lord of Shadows draws his power from the universe itself, in theory, if he was cut off from that source, then . . . I don't know, maybe."

"A vacuum in space might be the perfect prison," I said, my mind spinning.

Eleni looked doubtful. "If Shangó had found a way to trap the Lord of Shadows, we wouldn't be having this conversation."

I shifted on my heels, uneasy about the whole thing. Maybe I was reading too much into Shangó's theories on dark energy, and they had nothing to do with the Lord of Shadows. "There's only one way to find out."

After a while, the orishas disappeared—all except Oshun.

She transformed her outfit into a velvety pink tracksuit with rose-gold stripes down the sides of the legs and arms. She wore a matching headscarf to tie back her braids. "Training starts in five minutes, godlings!"

"Why do we have to practice if Yemoja is sending us to Azur?" Winston groaned as he, Candace, and Tay jumped down from the bleachers. Several kids had flocked to him since this morning, after his big speech about squaring up against the Lord of Shadows. Part of me wanted to tell everyone the truth, how he almost got himself killed, but we had bigger problems.

"I think you missed the part about the celestials' plan not being foolproof," I said. "They've fought the Lord of Shadows twice before and barely defeated him."

"Their plan won't work," Zeran said matter-of-factly. "He's too strong."

Winston glanced to Tisha Thomas, who stood in his growing group of friends. "I suppose you should know."

"From my understanding, the darkbringers almost got the best of you this morning." Oshun snapped her fingers, and four lights of different colors divided the gym. A number flashed in the air above each section—blue for the fifth graders, yellow for the sixth graders, green for the seventh graders, and orange for the eighth graders. "You will be safe on Azur, but it's my intention to make sure you are prepared to defend yourself if it comes to that."

"In case you didn't notice, we kicked darkbringer butt today," Winston said, and several kids cheered and clapped.

Oshun turned her razor-sharp smile on him. "I'd think that you children would have figured it out already. The darkbringers you fought were a distraction while the Lord of Shadows made his move. You didn't defeat them. They left once they'd completed their tasks."

I looked around at the faces of my fellow godlings. We were 143. Our entire community couldn't be more than 500 godlings if I counted both adults and children. Even if all the godlings gathered from across the human world, we'd still be outnumbered like a million to one. Maybe it wouldn't matter in the end, but I still wanted to train. I had a feeling that I wasn't the only one.

Once the godlings had settled in their designated areas, the gym transformed into multiple levels. We could see the sixth graders above us through a transparent floor and the fifth graders two levels up. The eighth graders were a floor beneath us. Each grade occupied a different space, so we could all practice at once. Neat trick.

"Pick a partner and defend yourself," Oshun said, her voice easily projecting over the group. "I have erected safeguards in the gym to lessen the effects of magic that might be dangerous."

"What's the point then?" someone murmured behind me. "Ogun never did that."

The orisha of beauty narrowed her eyes. "It should be obvious that I am not Ogun. My brother is the god of war and, as such, prefers brute force in an attack. Today I will teach you the art of subtlety."

Frankie teamed up with Eli, and Zeran paired off with me. The last time we fought, Zeran and I were tied at one win each. It felt a little silly to still keep score, but it also was nice to think about something other than leaving our neighborhood or our impending doom. This would be the last time we'd practice at JMS, at least for a while, and I would miss the worn bleachers, the faded lines on the basketball court, and the trophies in the hallways.

"No weapons allowed," Oshun said in her singsong voice. "Rule number one: rely on your natural abilities."

"Sorry," I said, consoling the shuddering ring on my finger.

Oshun cleared her throat. "Rule number two: expect the unexpected." She waved her hand, and white ribbons wound through the gym and spun us around until we were facing new opponents.

I stood across from Winston, who grinned like a cat about to pounce on a mouse. Eli faced off against Candace, and Frankie had Tay as her new sparring partner. Zeran squared up against Maurice Miller, who looked sleepy even though he'd been sleeping in class earlier today.

"You're not so tough without your little staff," Winston

said, blue flares dancing on his fingers. "I haven't forgotten about how you and your friends made me look bad at the beginning of the school year."

"Good." I gave him my most cutting glare. "And I haven't forgotten about all the times you bullied me and called me names, or what you said about my family."

Winston blasted streaks of fire at me one after another. I ducked, but his flames anticipated my move. The first one changed its trajectory and hit me in my chest. The second one slammed into my shoulder. When did he learn that trick? Harmless puffs of smoke drifted up from my shirt.

"Look at the guardian of the veil now—what a joke." Winston doubled over laughing. "You'd be ashes if Oshun didn't limit our magic."

He sent another fireball straight for me, but this time I was ready. I raised my hands, palms facing out. In a split second, sparks of light flashed before my eyes, and a mini-gateway opened in front of me.

The fireball changed path like before, but the gateway moved quickly to intercept. When the two collided, the fireball disappeared. Gritting his teeth, Winston shot more flames from his fingertips. I opened a second and a third gateway. I was drenched in sweat, but I was proud of myself. I was holding my own. And I'd finally learned how to open multiple gateways at once. Maybe it was the threat of being burned to a crisp.

Winston groaned and ran at me. I didn't have time to think as one of my gateways grew in size. The roaring vortex spun with glowing god symbols around the outer ring, and the middle was darker than the darkest night.

"What the heck?" Winston screamed. He tried to stop, but his momentum carried him forward. As he teetered on the edge of falling in, I felt a strange pull from the gateway, like it was calling to me. I stepped toward it, and I stumbled as I drew closer.

"That's enough, Maya," Oshun said, cutting through the fog in my head. Her ribbons yanked Winston back.

I lost my concentration, and the gateway dissipated like a cloud of smoke.

Winston was on the floor, glaring up at me in disgust. He climbed to his feet. "You tried to send me into the Dark, didn't you? All that talk about being on the same side and you do something so underhanded. I shouldn't be surprised. Who's afraid of the Lord of Shadows destroying our world when we have Maya?"

"I—I didn't," I stuttered. "That wasn't the Dark . . . It was . . . it was someplace else." *Someplace worse*, said a little voice in the back of my mind.

"Whatever, Maya," Winston spat. "For all we know, you're one of the Lord of Shadows' spies too."

Anger burned in my chest. How dare he question my loyalty? Oshun caught my eye, and everyone else in the gym faded to the background, like she and I had been removed from time. "Even with my wards in place, you opened a gateway into another dimension. That shouldn't have been possible. Had I not intervened, Winston might have found himself in grave danger."

"It was a mistake," I said quietly. "I didn't mean to do it."

"Haven't you made enough mistakes, Maya?" Oshun shook her head. "Perhaps you should sit out the rest of the training to think about the error of your ways."

Suddenly we were back in real time, and Oshun turned to the other godlings. "Rule number three: if you cannot control your abilities, then you are a danger to yourself and those around you."

I crossed my arms, frustrated. "You're just making these rules up as you go."

"Take a seat, Maya." Oshun pointed to the bleachers, then while still staring me down, she added, "Rule number four: never underestimate your opponent."

I stormed to the bleachers. I didn't need Winston accusing me of being a spy and Oshun reminding me of my mistakes. I watched the matches for a while before my mind began to wander. I thought about Shangó's equations again.

If I could open gateways into other dimensions without even trying, then maybe I could trap the Lord of Shadows outside the universe. I sank against the bleachers. Not that Papa would even let me attempt it.

"What makes you think you can succeed where the celestials have failed?" I mumbled to myself.

I bit back my doubt. Someone had to try. We had to strike now while the Lord of Shadows was still trapped in the library. That said, I'd already broken so many rules, and I had promised not to keep secrets from Papa. I decided then that I would tell him about Shangó's theory. Yemoja was right about one thing: celestials and godlings needed to work together to defeat the Lord of Shadows.

I cracked my knuckles, determined. It was time to finally put an end to the Lord of Shadows and his diabolical plans.

SIXTEEN

THE KING OF PETTINESS

I SAT ON THE bleachers with my arms crossed until Oshun finally dismissed the other godlings. When Winston passed by me on the way to the locker room, he rubbed his eyes and made a weeping sound before bursting into laughter with his friends. "Poor, Maya. Still don't know how to control your powers."

I tried to push down my anger. I wouldn't let him rattle me like he had in English class. I had more pressing things to worry about than his taunts.

"Don't forget rule number three," Winston added, pulling off his best imitation of Oshun's singsong voice. "If you cannot control your abilities, then you are a danger to yourself and those around you."

He and his friends laughed again—all except Candace,

Tisha, and a few others, who looked down at their shoes. Even they seemed sick of his antics. I didn't get him, like, at all. We were in the middle of the biggest crisis the human world had ever seen, and he still had the energy to pick a fight with me.

"It was a good thing that Oshun stopped Maya in time," Zeran said as he, Frankie, Eli, and Eleni came to my rescue. "Otherwise, Winston, you'd be joining Eli's army of ghosts."

"Oh, no, not happening." Eli threw up his arms and backed away. "I don't let rejects into my army. My standards are much higher, and unfortunately, Winston, you don't meet the minimum requirements."

Winston glared at Eli, then gave me an equally vicious look. "One of these days after this crap with the Lord of Shadows is over, I'm going to crush you like the bugs you are."

"We'll try not to hold our breath," I said dismissively.

Winston grimaced and turned to his friends. "Let's go. We have better things to do than waste time on these losers."

When they were gone, Eleni shook her head. "That boy is quite annoying."

"Quite," Frankie said.

At least Winston thought there would be a life *after* the Lord of Shadows. He hadn't given up hope either. Though he still didn't get that we were on the same side, fighting for the same thing. Bickering among ourselves was a bad look.

"I have something I need to do," Zeran announced suddenly. "I'll see you all tomorrow."

I had *almost* forgotten Tisha's warning about Zeran betraying me. If he was a spy, why would he have helped us defeat the darkbringers or fend off the Lord of Shadows? Well, unless he was deep undercover, meaning he would do anything to pretend to be on our side until the very last moment, then BAM, betrayal.

As Zeran set off, I pushed the thought out of my mind. I couldn't sit around and worry about what might happen with him when we had the Lord of Shadows to deal with right now.

"I cannot believe that darkbringer had the nerve to snatch my ghosts from me," Eli said once we were on our way home. "Who does *Carran* think she is?"

Eleni dipped her chin into her fluffy scarf and pulled the hood of her coat over her head. Her skin looked almost frozen. "Oshun said that the darkbringers attacked the school to distract us while the Lord of Shadows broke through the veil. He must've sent Auntie Tyana as a distraction too."

A squirrel scurried through the tree branches as we passed, and a dusting of snow fell on our heads. Eli laughed, but I got a chill down my back. Eleni squeaked as if she'd been sprayed by a skunk. Frankie didn't seem to notice. She stared ahead with her eyebrows pinched, and I could tell that she had something on her mind.

The squirrel leaped from one tree to the next. It was almost like it was following us. All this business with the Lord of Shadows had me paranoid.

"Maybe it wouldn't be so bad to spend time on Azur," said Eleni. "The weather is always perfect there."

"Speaking of Azur." Frankie snapped out of her daze. "I'm wondering who I can ask about the Azurians in the photo with my mother."

Eleni frowned for a moment, then her eyes got big. "Perhaps you can start at the Great Library. If I recall correctly, it contains the history of the universe. If the three people in the photo were fugitives, then there may be some mention in the archives."

Frankie bit her lip. "I hope so."

I was worried about her. If it were me, I'd want closure too. She deserved to know what happened to her first mom, but it wouldn't make her feel better. Mama always said that sometimes we had to face the things that scared us, but that didn't always mean monsters. Sometimes the truth was scary, but we still had to be brave and not run away from it.

***

Later that night, Mama and Eleni bustled around the kitchen making dinner while I nervously waited for Papa to get home. It almost felt like before, when I didn't know he was the guardian of the veil and he'd be gone all the time. I had been nervous then too.

When Papa finally arrived and we all sat down for dinner, he and Mama started talking about the evacuation. Eleni pushed chunks of roasted potatoes around her plate. I poked at my green beans and waited for an opening in their conversation to talk about Shangó's dark energy equations.

"We'll have most of the humans in the neighborhood moved out by tomorrow afternoon," Papa was saying. "They've been told that there's a toxic leak and that the relocation will be temporary."

Mama glanced up from her plate, surprised. "And they believed that?"

"Everyone but Mr. Mason." Papa leaned back against his chair and shrugged. "He swears it's a government conspiracy to replace him with a robot."

"Hmm," Mama said absently, then she added, "I'll be helping Nana evacuate all the godlings and their families to Azur."

"We can help too," I volunteered.

Eleni sat up straighter. "Yes, we'd be glad to."

Mama looked at us like we'd both grown a third eye in the center of our foreheads. "Children will be in the first groups we send to Azur, and that includes you both," she said. "No exceptions."

"But, Mama—"

She quirked an eyebrow, and my protest died before I could get it out. It was no use. When Mama had her mind made up, there was no changing it. After an awkward silence, she drew in a deep breath, and her face softened. "Maya, honey, you and Eleni have gone through so much already. You've both been so brave, but now it's time to let the adults deal with the Lord of Shadows."

Eleni quietly shoved green beans in her mouth and chewed slowly, like it was all she could do to keep from saying something.

"Your mother's right," Papa added as he pushed aside his plate. "We won't be able to hold back the Lord of Shadows much longer. When he breaks out of the library, he will attempt to destroy everyone and everything in his path. It's up to me and the other celestials to find a way to stop him."

When he breaks out of the library, not *if.* The fork slipped from my hand and crashed against my plate. The celestials already knew that their plan would fail.

"How . . . how long do we have?" Eleni asked, her voice full of hesitation.

Papa stared at his hands, contemplating. "A week, maybe two at the most, though we've underestimated the Lord of Shadows too many times to count."

"He draws energy from the universe, right?" I asked, rushing my words. "Could dark energy be used to create a vacuum in space to cut him off from his power source?"

"I wish it were that simple." Papa pinched the bridge of his nose and closed his eyes briefly. "Even if we could create a vacuum, it would still exist within the universe."

I slouched in my chair. I was sure Shangó's theory would be the answer, but it was a dead end.

"What if we all left earth?" Eleni looked up at Papa with fat tears in her eyes. "You and the other celestials could move everyone to another planet or even another dimension."

Papa and Mama exchanged a sad glance, and I held my breath, prepared for more bad news. "Celestials and godlings might be able to come and go between worlds, but humans can't, not without us changing the essence of what they are. They would be transformed in ways that no one could anticipate."

Last summer, Miss Lucille had told Frankie, Eli, and me about how the darkbringers came to exist. Obatala and Oduduwa made the darkbringers along with other magical creatures. But the universe had already seeded life on earth in the form of sea slugs, and the darkbringers were accidentally destroying it. The celestials hadn't anticipated that. Then again when Papa created the veil, it had devastating effects on the darkbringers. The celestials hadn't foreseen that either.

"I don't understand, Papa." Eleni frowned. "It doesn't matter if you change humans if you can save their lives."

"I think I do," I said quietly. "If the celestials change

humans, we don't know what will happen. They might end up repeating the same mistake they made with the dark-bringers."

"We haven't ruled it out," Papa said. "We're saving it as the last option, although I can't say for certain that the Lord of Shadows will not follow us no matter how far we go."

"Why would he follow us if all humans, celestials, and godlings alike left earth?" Mama asked. "He'll have what he wants."

Eleni stabbed a potato with her fork. "The Lord of Shadows is the king of pettiness."

I stared down at my plate. We were back to the same problem. The Lord of Shadows would break out of the library soon, and no one knew how to stop him.

SEVENTEEN

SWEET DREAMS

AFTER DINNER, I had a hard time falling asleep. I lay in bed thinking about how everything had gone terribly wrong. The Lord of Shadows was always one step ahead of us. He might be stuck in the library for now, but he must have a bigger plot brewing. That was why he'd sent Captain Nulan through the veil ahead of time. Luckily, we'd been there to stop her.

I kept imagining the Lord of Shadows in his cocoon, wrapped in layers of writing shadows that thrashed around on the library floor. He was biding his time, waiting patiently. Papa's words replayed in my mind: *When he breaks out of the library, he will attempt to destroy everyone and everything in his path.*

When I opened my eyes again, I was standing in front

of the old house on Fiftieth Street. My friends and I passed it every day on our way to school. It has been a sprawling mansion once; now it was covered in vines and mold, and all the windows were boarded up. The boards had been spray-painted over so many times with street art that it all blended together.

No one had ever lived in it that I could remember. Even squatters avoided it like the plague. I had stood here once before, in what I had thought was a dream, with Eli and Frankie, but it hadn't been a dream. I had been on the crossroads—the place between worlds, where dreams intersect with reality.

I clutched the rusted gate, feeling the grit underneath my fingers. The yard was blanketed in fog that completely covered the grass. My ring pulsed, and the symbols vibrated. I was frozen in place, my eyes glued to the darkness now spilling from the open door. The house began to rattle and creak like a monster waking up from a long slumber.

"You have such a wandering mind, Maya" came a low, slippery voice. "Your father should've done a better job of teaching you how to protect it."

I squeezed the fence harder, and the metal glowed underneath my hands. Papa had taught me how to keep the crossroads at bay if I concentrated hard enough, but it wasn't working now. Instead, the yard between me and the old house was shrinking.

"You're not really here," I said through gritted teeth. "You *can't* be."

Purple and black ribbons clambered out of the door—at first a few, then a dozen, then two dozen. The Lord of Shadows' violet eyes shined bright against the darkness like satellites in the night sky. "I am tired, Maya," he said, and he sounded very ancient, like he was glass on the verge of shattering. "This war must end now for me to truly rest."

"This war doesn't need to *happen*," I said, doing my best to sound brave. "The darkbringers are okay now. Why start another war that will kill countless people when you could let the past go?"

"I cannot fault you for being so naive," the Lord of Shadows said, his ribbons climbing across the porch and down the stairs. "You think that I do this only out of revenge, but it isn't that simple. It never is. This world belongs to the darkbringers. It always has, but your father and the others pushed them aside to make way for humankind. That cannot stand. It cannot go unpunished. For every action there is a reaction, a repercussion. That is the very nature of the universe."

"You would let innocent people die so you can punish the celestials?" I asked. "Haven't enough lives been lost already?"

"I'm only getting started," he spat. "I'm going to reshape the universe in my own image."

There it was. His true purpose. For all his talk about avenging the darkbringers, it came down to one thing: the Lord of Shadows was just like all the other power-hungry, diabolical, evil overlords with no regard for anyone but themselves. He was no different from the bad guys Oya faced in her comic books. No matter what I said to him, he'd find a way to justify his actions. I couldn't believe that I ever thought he could be reasoned with. "Eleni was right; you are the king of petty," I said under my breath.

The Lord of Shadows propelled himself through the doorway, the darkness peeling back from his moon face. He floated on his hundreds of ribbons. "I don't need both you and Eleni alive."

I tried to pull back from the fence as the Lord of Shadows drew closer, but I was stuck in place. I remembered what Papa said last summer.

Maya, listen to me. If you ever see the Lord of Shadows again in your dreams, run and find a place to hide.

But what can he do in a dream? I'd asked.

He can kill.

"It is really a shame that you must die." The Lord of Shadows was halfway across the yard, gliding forward on a pile of his ribbons. "I wouldn't have gotten this far without your help. In a way, I owe you my gratitude."

"You have a funny way of showing you're grateful," I said, my voice laced with sarcasm. "How about you stop trying to kill everybody, and we'll call it even? Deal?"

"Perhaps if you weren't my enemy's spawn, I would consider sparing you," the Lord of Shadows said, brushing off my offer. "But it gives me great pleasure to break your father little by little." His lips curled into a snarl, and his violet-colored eyes darkened. "Eleggguá will be devastated to lose his *baby girl*."

The way he spat out the words *baby girl* made my skin crawl. As if I hadn't realized before now that the Lord of Shadows didn't have a remorseful bone in his body. That was if he even had bones. It was more likely that under those ribbons was a sack of cow dung.

"I am doing the world a favor," he droned on without pause. "You are a dangerous girl, Maya Janine Abeola. The celestials just don't know it yet. I can sense that you have the potential to reshape the universe, if not destroy it altogether. How ironic."

His ribbons struck me. It happened so fast that I stumbled, dazed. Instinctively, I curled my hand, thinking I had my staff, but my fingers only dug into my palm. I was so cold, like someone had thrust me into a deep freezer. The pain came at once. Stabbing, excruciating pain. My leg buckled, but before I could hit the ground, the Lord of Shadows had wrapped his ribbons around my chest.

I couldn't breathe.

I gasped for air, my lungs burning, but nothing came.

"It's a mercy that I kill you now," the Lord of Shadows croaked as my vision faded in and out. "Goodbye, Maya."

"Put her down," someone shouted.

When my eyes came back into focus, Eleni stood beside me with fairy magic swirling around her at a dizzying pace. When it landed on the ribbons, they shrieked and drew back. The fence started to glow brighter, and the light reflected off the gold and amber in Eleni's hair. "I'm not going to let you hurt my sister," she said, her eyes narrowed. "You already took Mama, Kimala, and Genu. I won't let you take her, too." She reached out her hand and helped me get to my feet. "Are you okay?"

"Never better." I bit back my pain. "How . . . how are you in my dream?" Not that I was complaining. I'd be double-burned toast right now if she hadn't shown up.

"I'm not in your dream," she said, frowning. "You're in *mine, aren't you?*"

Well, that didn't make any sense. Was this the real Eleni or a dream version of my sister created by my subconscious mind? "Maybe our minds somehow intersected on the crossroads," I said reluctantly.

The Lord of Shadows growled as he shot his ribbons out again. This time toward both Eleni and me, but they stopped short. Eleni was shaking as she clutched the fence hard. Her fairy magic was fading fast. She wouldn't be able to keep this up for long. "Some help, please," she said. "We can close the door to the crossroads if we work together."

I rushed back to the fence, but I tripped over my feet and fell against it. Clumsiness aside, I concentrated on the door to the old house. That was how the Lord of Shadows had snuck into my (and apparently Eleni's) dream. He always had another trick up his sleeve. No wonder the celestials hadn't been able to stop him. It didn't help that he fought dirty.

My magic added to Eleni's, and the fence glowed brighter. The Lord of Shadows shrank back, with his ribbons fanning around him in disarray. For a moment, we couldn't see him. Then the ribbons peeled away to reveal an aziza boy a little taller than Eleni. He had red-and-purple semitransparent wings with yellow along the edges. His eyes were large and round in a way that reminded me of a lost puppy.

"What happened to us being friends forever, Eleni?" he said in an innocent voice. "Don't you remember that you opened the gateway to save *me*?"

Fat tears rolled down Eleni's cheeks, but she didn't falter. She looked at me, and I said, "It's time to shut this nightmare down."

Eleni tilted up her chin. "I quite agree, Sister."

Together we concentrated our energy on building more light. In his kid form, the Lord of Shadows roared at us, screaming in pain. He backed onto the porch, step by step.

"When this is over, I will get rid of you both," he said before fading back into the house. The door slammed shut behind him.

"Not today you won't," Eleni said. "*Not ever.*"

"The Abeola sisters: one," I said, feeling drained. "The Lord of Shadows: a big, empty zero."

"We did it," Eleni cheered, still facing the old house.

I slipped to the ground to rest and closed my eyes. I could hear the echo of Eleni urgently calling my name. "Maya, are you okay?"

I woke to ear-piercing screams. My heart slammed against my chest, and I was drenched in sweat. *Eleni.* I had to get to my sister. Had the Lord of Shadows doubled back on the crossroads? I tried to climb out of bed, but I couldn't. Why was my throat so raw?

I yanked back my blanket, then I saw it. Gray ash spread across my chest where the Lord of Shadows had attacked me in my dream. But I couldn't worry about that—I had to help my sister. Only, it took my brain too long to register my grave miscalculation. It wasn't Eleni screaming. *It was me.*

EIGHTEEN

What if something goes wrong?

To say that my life flashed before my eyes would be an understatement. I stared in shock as my hands turned from brown to ash gray. Searing pain cut across my chest, and I squeezed my eyes shut. I inhaled, but even the air burned my lungs. I clenched my hands into fists, but again, the pain only grew worse. It couldn't end this way.

My tombstone would read, *Here lies Maya Janine Abeola, guardian of the veil in training, bested by the sinister Lord of Shadows, enemy to all.* Or would it read, *Here lies Maya Janine Abeola, guardian of the veil in training, who let the Lord of Shadows outsmart her?* I could think of a thousand ways to say what basically came down to this fact: the Lord of Shadows had dealt me the death blow.

"Maya, breathe, baby girl," Papa said. His voice was soothing, calm.

I latched on to my father's words like they were a lifeline. I could feel warm light wash over me, and the pain began to lessen. When I opened my eyes, he was sitting on the side of my bed. Mama sat on the opposite side, stroking my hair and blinking back tears. Eleni stood nearby with her arms wrapped around her.

"The Lord of Shadows . . ." I groaned.

Papa squeezed my hand. "He can't hurt you now."

Mama pressed a cool towel to my forehead, just like she used to do when I was little and had a dizzy spell. It always helped me feel better. "How are you feeling, baby?"

I held up my hands, afraid that my fingers had turned to ash and fallen off, but I counted all ten digits. "Better now that Eleni and I closed the door to the crossroads."

Eleni rocked on her heels. "Let's keep it closed this time."

We didn't agree on everything or have the same taste in clothes, but this was something we could agree on. I never wanted to see the crossroads again. *Ever.* "Thanks for saving my butt."

"That's what sisters are for," she said, flashing me a huge smile. "That and occasionally share clothes."

I'd rather share clothes any day than deal with the Lord of Shadows.

"I'll feel better once you both are in Azur." Mama's tone was firm, but her voice was tired and wary. "You'll be safe there."

"No place's safe from *him*," Eleni mumbled.

"It's safer than here," Papa said, coming to his feet. "For now."

"Are you sure you're okay, Maya?" Mama asked again, looking me over for any signs of trouble. "I was going to help with the evacuation today, but I can stay home."

"I'm fine, Mama," I insisted, not wanting to derail her plans. "Besides, Eleni will be here with me."

"I'll make you chestnut and watercress soup!" Eleni volunteered. "My mother used to make it for me when I was sick."

"I'm not sick," I moaned.

"I know, but you *are* recuperating!"

"No more fixing tears in the veil, okay?" Papa said. "Pack your things and be ready to leave tomorrow morning."

I opened my mouth to protest, but Papa shook his head. That was the end of that. Did all parents have a talent for shutting down conversations so quickly? My parents were masters at it.

Once Mama and Papa left, Eleni went downstairs to the kitchen. I climbed out of bed and stared out the window. It was still morning, but a dark cloud had settled over the neighborhood. Across the street, movers packed my ex-babysitter Latesha's art into the back of a white van. One of the movers carried a stop sign painted neon green, with bottle caps and paperclips glued onto it. Another one was balancing a tower made of plates and forks.

"Be careful with that," Latesha said to the man with the plates. "That piece took me ten months to finish."

There were moving vans parked on every corner as our human neighbors packed up their things. Latesha, LJ, Mr. Mason, the Campbells, the Patels, the Lees. They were all leaving, and soon the streets would be empty. I pressed my hand against the cold window, and a chill shot through my shoulders. The Lord of Shadows had already started to destroy our neighborhood.

"May I come in?" Zeran asked from behind me.

I turned around too fast and got a little dizzy. "Sure."

"I heard what happened," he said, standing in my doorway. "You okay?"

I shrugged and held up my hand to show him. "I got my color back."

Zeran began to pace in circles until he stopped in front of a pile of *Oya: Warrior Goddess* comics. He picked up the latest edition and frowned. He'd read some of the older editions that I let him borrow. "I hope I get to read the rest. Oya reminds me a little of you. Brave, fierce, a little unpredictable."

Was he blushing? Tell me he wasn't blushing. "Um, thanks."

Zeran glanced up from the comic book. "So . . ."

It was time to come clean about Tisha Thomas's vision. It wasn't right to keep it a secret, even if I had my doubts. "Tisha said that you would betray me to save your brother," I blurted out.

Zeran stared at me, then let out a sharp laugh. "I know."

"What?" I said, surprised.

"Do you think you were the only person she told?"

"I guess." I frowned. "Why didn't you say anything?"

"I thought you would ask me if it was true, so I waited," he said. "When you never did, I figured you believed her."

I glanced away. "She saw it in a vision."

"I don't care what she saw, Maya." Zeran crossed his arms. "I don't betray my friends."

I blew out a deep breath. "Glad to hear it."

Zeran worked his lower jaw back and forth. "Tisha was right about one thing . . . I am going to save my brother."

"You're going back to the Dark?"

"No, he's not there . . . not anymore," Zeran admitted. "Eleni was right. The Lord of Shadows has been quietly gathering support from the magical creatures in the human world. Billu was assigned to one of the squads tasked with recruiting."

"How do you know this?"

Zeran dropped his arms to his side. He looked relieved to have someone to talk to. "Several key Resistance leaders have come over to the human world, too. They hope to undermine the Lord of Shadows before it's too late. I've been meeting with them to get information about Billu's whereabouts."

"Why didn't the Resistance contact the celestials?" I asked. "They should be working together to stop the Lord of Shadows."

"The Resistance doesn't trust the celestials . . . especially your father. He caused a lot of suffering when he created the veil."

My face burned with shame. Papa had never forgiven himself for the harm that he caused the darkbringers. "I know, but we have to work together if we want to stop a war from happening."

"I agree," Zeran said. "But they're not convinced."

"Where's your brother?"

Zeran grimaced, and his shoulders tensed. "I don't know yet . . . I'm supposed to meet someone this afternoon at that abandoned factory on Ashland. They'll tell me where Billu is in exchange for . . . *you*."

I narrowed my eyes at him. "You said you don't betray your friends."

"I don't." Zeran's face changed shape before my eyes. His skin turned from blue to brown, and he shrank by several inches. His hair grew into long locs. "How do I look?" he asked, grinning at me.

I gawked at him in disbelief. His shifting his appearance never got old, but it was eerie to look at a copy of myself, down to my clothes. I thought about Tisha's vision and connected the dots. "So you were going to pretend to be me and deliver yourself to the darkbringers?"

"Pretty good plan, right?" Zeran said in a voice that sounded exactly like mine. "Admittedly, it is going to be hard to pull off being in two places at once, but I'm resourceful."

Tisha Thomas had said she saw Zeran meeting with darkbringers in an old factory. Then she had a vision of me unconscious in said factory. Zeran *had* met with the darkbringers. So her vision hadn't been wrong. She'd just misinterpreted what she saw. I put my hands on my hips and smiled. "I'm going with you. You don't need to pretend to be me if I'm a willing accomplice."

Zeran shook his head. "It's too dangerous. If these people get their hands on you, they'll turn you over to the Lord of Shadows."

"Let me worry about that," I said. "You helped rescue my sister, so now let me help you get your brother back."

Zeran nodded slowly, like he was reluctant to agree, then he stepped closer to me. "You're all right for a human."

"And you're pretty okay for a darkbringer," I said, glancing at the floor.

"Maya, if . . . if the celestials can't stop the Lord of

Shadows, I want you to know . . ." Zeran paused, and his voice got low. "I want you to know that I'm glad to call you my friend."

Eleni cleared her throat, and Zeran and I jumped apart. She flounced into my room with a tray of steaming soup, animal crackers, and a glass of orange juice. "Should I come back later?"

"No," I said much too loudly. "We were just . . . *um* . . . talking."

"Uh-huh," Eleni said. "You two are planning to rescue Billu without the rest of us."

I pursed my lips, annoyed. "How long were you eavesdropping?"

Eleni put the tray on my desk. "I wasn't; I just happen to have really good hearing."

"I can't risk bringing more people," Zeran said. "If my contacts suspect a trap, they'll leave without telling me where to find my brother."

Eleni crossed her arms. "I don't like the idea of you two going alone. What if something goes wrong?"

"Then we'll deal with it," I told her. "Look, if I'm not home in time for dinner, tell Papa and Mama everything."

"Fine," Eleni said, throwing up her arms in defeat, "but you better come back *unharmed*."

"We don't have much time," Zeran said, shifting to his human form.

I grabbed my staff, and the first sparks of a gateway flashed before my eyes. "Old, spooky factory, here we come."

Zeran and I left Eleni behind, looking not too pleased. She'd get over it. We had to do this by the book if we wanted to find his brother. There was no room for error, and the more people involved, the bigger the chance that something would go wrong.

As soon as we exited the gateway, Zeran grabbed my arms and pinned them behind my back. He leaned in close to my ear. "Play along in case we're being watched." Then he raised his voice. "You should choose your friends more carefully, *godling*."

We were near the warehouse, and the building spanned almost an entire city block. I pretended to try to twist out of his grasp. "Traitor! I should have known better than to trust you."

Zeran shoved me, and I stomped on his foot for good measure. Soon, he was pushing me into the warehouse, where we'd play out our plan. "Did you have to stomp on my foot?"

"Got to make it look good," I said as we heard approaching steps from outside. "Sounds like they're here." I lay on the floor, which was covered in dust. I had to bury my nose in my jacket, so I didn't sneeze. I pretended to be unconscious, just like Tisha Thomas had seen in her vision.

A moment later, someone asked in a rough voice. "Is

that her . . . Elegguá's spawn?"

"The one and only," Zeran answered smugly.

"She's so . . . *tiny,*" another darkbringer chimed in. This one sounded like he had a stuffy nose.

I rolled my eyes beneath my jacket. He was in for a rude awakening. This *tiny* girl was about to kick his butt.

"I delivered the guardian as promised," Zeran said. "Now tell me how to find Billu."

"His squad was sent to Bayou Teche in Louisiana to convince the head of the adze, Black Mamba, to turn against the celestials," the first darkbringer answered. "They haven't been heard from since."

Zeran didn't say anything for a beat, and the silence was tense. His next words came out brittle. "No one went to look for them?"

"The Lord of Shadows does not tolerate failure," the darkbringer with the cold said. "He would not authorize resources to start a search, not even when your father insisted."

"Black Mamba lives on a sprawling estate at the end of Praline Road," said the first darkbringer. "You can't miss it, but if you value your life, you'll stay away."

"Let's take the girl and go," the second darkbringer declared as he kneeled beside me.

"About that." I jabbed my foot into his side. "Change of plans."

The darkbringer with the cold grabbed my throat, crushing my windpipe. The first darkbringer had turned his back to Zeran, still thinking that Zeran was on their side. His mistake. Zeran slipped one of the blue prods from under his sleeve and jammed it into his back. The darkbringer fell to the floor like a bag of rotten potatoes.

"Lights out," I squeaked between gasping for air.

The darkbringer who had me in a choke hold frowned right before he thought to look over his shoulder. Zeran smiled at him, then knocked him out with a shock from the prod. They were going to wake up with serious headaches.

"Who are these adze?" Zeran asked as he tied up the two darkbringers.

I swallowed hard, remembering Papa's stories about the adze. They were cunning, ruthless, and almost impossible to stop. They were creatures of the night. "They're vampires," I said quietly. "They feed off the blood of others to survive."

Zeran paced back and forth. "I shouldn't have left Billu behind. This is my fault."

I opened another gateway. "Let's go get your brother."

I only hoped that it wasn't too late.

NINETEEN

OPERATION RESCUE BILLU

THE GATEWAY SPAT us out on a narrow gravel road in the middle of Bayou Teche, and we were immediately besieged by the sound of croaking frogs and chirping crickets. Towering trees covered in Spanish moss cast shadows across the surrounding swamp. The air had the unmistakable rusty scent of blood mixed with wet wood and rotten fish. "Let's stay alert," I said, readying my staff. "Be prepared for anything."

Zeran slipped the prods from under his sleeves. "I'm always prepared."

Pockets of sunlight broke through the tree branches in some places, but we couldn't see more than a few feet in front of us. The symbols on my staff started to pulse frantically like it was warning us of the impending danger.

"Tell me more about these adze," Zeran said as we spotted a cluster of lights up ahead. "What are we up against?"

We started down the road, and I gave him a crash course in adze lore. "First of all, they're not your run-of-mill vampire. Crosses, garlic, holy water, sunlight, none of that stuff works against them. They're a different breed." I paused, and my voice dropped low. "According to legend, they prefer the blood of children. That's how they stay young." I bit my lip. "There's something else I'm forgetting . . ."

"What *does* work against them?" Zeran asked impatiently.

"They can only be defeated in their natural form," I said. "Otherwise, they're nearly invincible."

"What's their natural form?"

"Trust me, you'll know when you see it," I said as we tracked closer to the lights.

"Are you being vague on purpose?" Zeran groaned.

"I'm not being vague," I shot back. "I'm telling you what I know."

"Which isn't much," he snapped.

"I know more than you *obviously*!" I said through gritted teeth.

Zeran thrust one of his prods against my chest. "You're beginning to get on my nerves."

"Likewise." I knocked his prod away with my staff. "Maybe I should let you find your brother on your own."

"Fine!" Zeran said. "You were only pretending to be my friend anyway."

"And maybe you're a spy after all!" I said, accusing him, but then I frowned. This was all wrong. Why were we fighting? This didn't make sense. "Zeran, are you feeling irrationally angry?" I grimaced, finally remembering the thing I had forgotten about the adze. "Much like the aziza, the adze can influence a person's emotions, but they can only influence ones that cause chaos."

"Maya, watch out!" Zeran said, pushing me aside.

I hit the ground as he swung his prods at a cluster of fireflies that had been creeping up behind my back. They scattered for a moment but quickly started for us again. I would've smacked my forehead if I hadn't needed both hands. The other thing I forgot was that the adze could appear as fireflies, which was how they usually slipped into people's houses. One adze might be easy to defend against, but there were dozens of them buzzing around. "Don't let them touch you—they'll drink your blood."

Zeran rotated his wrist as he adjusted the prods. The electric hum from them grew louder, and I could feel the charge in the air. "These are the adze?"

"Yeah," I said, as the fireflies scattered again, but this time they retreated into the shadows.

Zeran helped me to my feet. "Is it just me, or does it feel like we're walking into a trap?"

I glanced ahead at the looming trees and the wrought-iron gate at the end of the road. "We are definitely walking into a trap."

Zeran rocked on his heels. "I won't blame you if you want to go back."

Before I could answer, a voice cooed, "Now y'all have come too far to turn into yellow-bellied chickens."

I squinted as the shadows peeled back from a tall man leaning against the gate, wearing a black fedora hat with a red feather. He had dark brown skin and a face so beautiful he could've been on magazine covers. He wore a plain white button-down shirt and matching trousers that looked much too hot for the bayou. "Are you Black Mamba?" I asked.

The man let out a hoarse laugh and stroked his chin. "I can see how you think that on account of my color, but alas, I'm the caretaker." When I frowned, he added, "I take care of the estate. Keep things tidy. Feed the gators."

"*Those gators*?" Zeran pointed at the shadows.

Four glowing eyes peered back at us, and I had to blink a few times to see the outlines of the alligators' bodies, if you could even call them that. They were the size of dragons. Since the adze didn't eat people like the elokos, only drank their blood, it wasn't hard to imagine what was on the dinner menu for the caretakers' pets.

"Black Mamba is expecting you," the caretaker drawled.

"Best not keep her waiting. She ain't particularly a patient woman."

All around us, the fireflies loomed in the shadows. They'd formed a circle, and I had no doubt that if we chose to flee, they'd attack before I had time to open a gateway.

"How did Black Mamba know we were coming?" Zeran demanded.

"Them two darkbringers said you'd bring the guardian." The caretaker answered like it was no concern of his. "Of course, they didn't say you'd be in cahoots with her." He laughed again, and it sounded like a dry cough. "No matter. Black Mamba always gets what she wants, and she wants the girl."

My heart was racing out of control. "And what does she want with me?"

"It ain't for me to say." The caretaker pushed himself away from the fence. Standing up straight, I saw that he was tall, even taller than Papa. His sideburns were curly against his face and shinier than any hair had the right to be. He swung open the gate, and it let out a long creak.

"Is my brother . . . is Billu . . ." Zeran couldn't finish his sentence.

The caretaker shrugged. "I don't get involved in Black Mamba's business."

One by one, the fireflies dimmed as the adze changed

their shapes in the shadows. They stalked around in the dark, and I caught glimpses of gray-specked skin, hunched backs, and talons sharp enough to cut a person in half in one swipe. The adze were massive, nothing like the dainty-looking vampires you saw in movies. These were the vampires of nightmares: bloodthirsty and ready for a snack.

The caretaker held up his hands in a peace gesture. "Easy now—let's not scare our guests."

"Let's go, Zeran," I said. "We have an appointment with Black Mamba whether we like it or not."

The caretaker slipped back into the shadows. "Good luck. Y'all going to need it."

Zeran and I exchanged a look as we entered the estate grounds. The trees were more tightly packed here, with so much moss that it was almost as dark as night. The light from my staff and Zeran's prods pushed back the shadows. It was eerily silent. No croaking frogs. No chirping crickets. No leaves rustling in the wind. Even animals had enough sense to stay away from this place, and here we were strolling up to the door.

We passed by a graveyard with ancient tombstones covered in vines. The three-story white house at the end of the driveway reminded me of those plantations you see in history class, which only gave me the creeps.

"Here we go," I said as we climbed the steps. My legs felt heavy.

Zeran pushed open the door, and it let out a low groan. Candles hung from sconces against the walls. We followed the narrow entranceway to a sitting room with red velvet chairs, brass accent tables, and vases with elaborate bouquets painted on them. It was old-school, emphasis on *old*. Heavy suits of armor stood in every corner. That wasn't weird at all—nope, not weird.

Classical music poured from a nearby room. The door was already ajar, and shadows flickered against a bookshelf. "Last chance to change your mind," Zeran whispered.

"No way," I said. "We're in this together."

"Well, then, perhaps you should come on in," croaked an ancient voice from inside the room. "I've been looking forward to meeting y'all."

Zeran eased out a breath, and I tightened my grip on the staff.

Here goes nothing. We stepped into the room. Black Mamba sat in a high-back chair, wearing a puffy blue dress that spread out around her feet. It was something that Eleni might have loved, but it was a few hundred years out of fashion. Black Mamba's long hair was in a single braid, and her skin was almost the same color as her hazel eyes. I had expected her to be more imposing, but she was barely taller than me and didn't look that much older. Being an immortal bloodsucker had done wonders for her skin.

We were in a library with bookshelves that stretched up

to the ceiling. Heavy, dark curtains hung at the tall windows, and a musty breeze filled the air. "Welcome, Zeran, brother of Billu," Black Mamba said with a Southern drawl, then she turned her attention to me. "Welcome, Maya, guardian of the veil. I've been expecting you."

Zeran stormed across the room toward Black Mamba. "Where's my brother?"

"I'm here" came another voice.

Billu was a mini version of Zeran with the same dark curly hair, deep-blue skin, and black wings. Zeran's shoulders sagged with relief to see his brother. "Are you okay?"

"I'm fine," Billu answered coldly.

"This is a time for celebration!" Black Mamba clapped her hands. "Brothers reunited and new alliances. With the Lord of Shadows' help, my people will no longer bow down to the celestials and their rules."

"You're making a mistake," I said, desperate. "The celestials have worked hard to find balance between the magical and nonmagical worlds. The Lord of Shadows wants chaos." As soon as the words left my mouth, I realized that it was a waste of breath. The adze seeded chaos, too. With the Lord of Shadows in control, they would get exactly what they wanted.

"We're leaving," Zeran said, then he turned to Black Mamba. "Don't try to stop us."

"I'm not going anywhere with you," Billu said. Spirals

of white smoke curled around him. "You don't care about me—you only care about yourself and *that girl*."

Billu thrust a finger in my direction, and a web shot out and slammed me against the wall. My staff hit the floor and rolled away.

"Billu, no!" Zeran said, but as he did, the white smoke curled into a giant monster.

"Laissez les bon temp rouler!" Black Mamba cheered. "*Let the good times roll!*"

I struggled to free myself from the spiderweb. It was ridiculous. The threads were so thin that I should've been able to punch through them, but they were strong. As I fought to free myself, new fibers sprouted from the threads.

Billu's smoke monster, which bore a striking resemblance to Godzilla, stood ten feet tall with three barbed tails and a row of sharp spines down its back that would put an impundulu to shame. It was the weirdest thing. I could see through the smoke as it swiveled around, but it was also solid in a way that defied logic. *Darkzilla* swept Zeran up with one claw and dangled him upside down by his ankle.

"Traitor!" Billu said, wiping away tears. Darkzilla roared in anguish, and I had a feeling that it was projecting Billu's emotions. "You don't belong with us. You belong with her kind. That's where your loyalties lie."

Billu looked to be nine or ten years old, and the way he talked made me think that his father, Commander Rovey, had said those things to him. I could understand why he was mad at Zeran. It must've seemed like his big brother had abandoned him.

"Billu," Zeran pleaded. "Remember that day when Father said that you would be joining the military, and you said you didn't want to? I promised that I would find a way to get you out."

"But you didn't!" Billu sniffled. Darkzilla roared, and the room shook. "You ran away and left me behind."

"I didn't run away!" Zeran whipped his tail at the monster's scaly paw. "I had to help Maya and her friends stop the Lord of Shadows from destroying the veil."

"Our lord wants to put the world back the way it's supposed to be," Billu said.

"No, Billu!" Zeran shouted. "He wants to start another war that will hurt a lot of people. You're smarter than this. Think for yourself. Don't let the Lord of Shadows trick you like he's done to Father and so many other people. A war would be bad for all sides—humans, godlings, darkbringers, even the celestials."

While Zeran and his brother argued, I had to find a way out of this cocoon. My hands were glued against my sides. I blinked, and Black Mamba was suddenly standing in front of me. "I was going to turn you over to the Lord of Shadows as a gift, but you smell too sweet." She smiled, and I saw rot between her teeth, which were sharpened into fine points.

"I'm going to enjoy drinking the blood of a godling."

I swallowed hard and said the first thing that came to mind. "You don't want to drink my blood; it tastes like vinegar."

Black Mamba leaned in close to me and laughed. "I shall soon see."

TWENTY

BLOODLUST

As Black Mamba moved in for the kill, her teeth grew longer and sharper. If only I could get one arm loose from the web, one hand, one finger even. I didn't want to go down without a fight. Black Mamba was two seconds from sinking her teeth into my throat when Zeran launched one of his prods. It slammed into her back, and electricity buzzed in the air. Black Mamba's whole body went stiff as the prod clanked against the floor. Once she regained control of herself, she whirled around.

Zeran was still hanging upside down. Billu's Darkzilla monster dangled him by his ankles. "Did I get your attention?"

"You shouldn't have done that," Black Mamba hissed. Her nails grew into long talons, and the shadow she cast in the room was suddenly tall, lumbering, and hunched over. She stalked toward Zeran, taking her sweet time. "I have curbed my appetite, but perhaps I shall have my first taste of darkbringer blood tonight, too."

"You can't have my brother!" Billu shouted. "You said that you'd free me and the other recruits once he brought the guardian. You have what you want. Leave him alone."

Okay, Real Talk: The Lord of Shadows was wrong for sending a bunch of children to win over the adze, especially since the adze consumed the blood of children to stay young. It was almost like he had sent them as gifts to Black Mamba. Of all the low-down, dirty things to do, this was the bottom of the bottom.

"I've changed my mind, little boy," Black Mamba snarled. "You children have enough blood to sustain my youth for centuries to come."

"Billu, let me go!" Zeran said, but his brother was already in motion.

Darkzilla quickly lowered Zeran to the floor as Black Mamba launched herself at them. She was a blur of puffy blue dress as she practically flew across the room. Billu's Darkzilla moved between her and the brothers, but she dug her talons into its smoke belly and tore right through it.

Zeran pushed his brother to the side, then he tucked his chin against his chest, his eyes narrowed. Random objects in the room started to shake and fly toward each other. A pile of chairs, lamps, paintings, vases, and other furniture stacked itself in the center of the room. Zeran's power was similar to his brother's, but it manifested by using objects around him. It was the same as what happened at the garbage dump when we fought Captain Nulan. The pile melted together, taking shape into a beast. Black Mamba leaped on top of the half-melted furniture and flung herself at Zeran. She slammed into him, knocking him to the floor. The various pieces of furniture that had formed his monster fell apart.

"No," Billu screamed, and his Darkzilla began to unravel. Billu raced toward his brother, but Black Mamba backhanded him across the face and sent him flying across the room.

All of this happened in seconds, and I was half in shock. I had to snap out of it. We weren't about to die in the middle of the bayou. My friend was in trouble, and I was still struggling to get out of the cocoon. I concentrated on my staff at my feet. "A little help, please," I begged, but a gush of wind came through the window and rolled the staff farther away.

I thought about our lesson with Oshun. Rule number one: *rely on your natural abilities*. I'd sparred against Winston without my staff and almost lost control of my magic. I couldn't afford to make that mistake again. Not with so much on the line.

I looked on in horror as Zeran swung his remaining

prod at Black Mamba. The electric current from the weapon buzzed, but she was too quick and stayed out of his reach. Suddenly, she began to change into the lumbering thing I saw in her shadows—a creature with speckled gray skin and tufts of black hair across her back. This was her true form. When she was in her most dangerous state. She swept her claw through the air and cut Zeran's prod in half. He rolled out of the way in time to miss her next blow.

It was now or never. I had to trust myself to use my magic without my staff. I concentrated on opening a gateway beneath my feet, and soon I was falling. I bit back a scream as the god symbols spun around me in a frenzy. I was careening toward a bottomless pit. I had to regain control.

I shifted my mind back to Zeran and Black Mamba, and slowly the symbols in the gateway settled. I landed with a thud, still in the library. My whole body ached, but the cocoon had fractured on impact. I climbed to my feet and scooped up my staff just as Billu was coming to. He groggily rubbed his eyes. Zeran was holding his own against Black Mamba, but he was losing ground. He was bleeding from a cut on his arm that thankfully only looked like a claw mark, not teeth. A bite would be the kiss of death.

"Hey, Black Mamba," I called. "I believe we have some unfinished business."

Black Mamba raised her lopsided head and bared her teeth at me. The whites of her eyes swirled with blood as she flung out an arm and knocked Zeran aside. She was done with him for the time being.

Growling, she bounded toward me, her talons poised and ready to strike. I crouched and spun around, sweeping the staff in one wide arc. When the staff connected with her, the god symbols rearranged themselves. The infinity symbol, the moon, and lightning peeled away from the staff and flew into her. I didn't pretend to know what all the symbols meant, but if the infinity symbol was involved, it had something to do with longevity or old age, depending on the context. The impact sent her crashing into one of the bookshelves.

I froze when she quickly got back to her feet, but she took one step and fell to her knees. Her gray skin began to wrinkle. "No," she screamed as she scratched herself hard enough to draw blood. Ouch. "This cannot be! I am eternal."

I realized then what the symbols must have done. "You were eternal, but not anymore," I said as she collapsed to the floor. Her skin shriveled until it looked like sun-beaten leather. She'd drunk the blood of countless people to stay young, and now she looked her true age. I almost felt sorry for her. *Almost.* By the end, she was nothing but a dusty corpse, her chest barely moving as she breathed in and out.

"Whoa, is she . . ." Billu asked from behind me.

I turned around and faced Zeran's little brother. He

had been a ball of rage and anger only minutes ago, but now, he looked confused. He stared at me with huge black eyes. "No, she's in a state of hibernation, and without blood, she'll stay that way indefinitely."

Zeran got to his feet. No denying that he'd just gone toe to toe with an adze and lived to tell the story. He was covered in bruises. "I would never abandon you, Billu," he said, his voice choked with tears. "We're brothers."

Billu's lips quivered as he stared up at Zeran. The two of them stood across from each other for a full minute before Billu broke into sobs and hugged him. "I thought I would never see you again."

Zeran ruffled his brother's hair with his knuckles. "We have a lot to catch up on, but for now, we need to free the other recruits."

"They're here," Billu said as he jogged over to one of the bookshelves. He pulled a lever forward, and the shelf clicked as a hidden door unlatched. "Down in the basement. Black Mamba put them there. She said they were her insurance policy in case one of us double-crossed her."

"Go ahead. I'll keep watch," I said. "We need to get out of here before the other adze figure out what's happened to Black Mamba."

While Zeran and Billu headed down the stairs behind the bookshelf, I locked the heavy double doors to the room—not that I thought it would really stop an adze, but it seemed like the sensible thing to do.

No sooner had I locked the door than a loud, slow clap rang out. The caretaker was perched on a windowsill in a corner when he hadn't been there only a moment ago. Scratch that: in his firefly form, he could have slipped into the room at any time during our fight with Black Mamba. "Congratulations," he said, his voice full of delight. "I have been waiting a very long time for this day."

"Huh?" I shifted into a defensive stance in case he decided to attack. "You wanted me to defeat Black Mamba?"

The caretaker gave one of his hoarse laughs, and a chill shot down my spine. "I'm Black Mamba now." He straightened his collar. "The name suits me, don't you think?"

I frowned. "I don't understand."

"Black Mamba is a title held by the leader of our enclave," the caretaker explained. "When the previous Black Mamba is otherwise incapacitated, another must take their place."

"And you're that one . . ."

The caretaker . . . *um*, the new Black Mamba smiled, revealing very sharp teeth. "My predecessor was going to keep you all for herself, but I plan to share with my siblings."

Zeran, Billu, and the recruits bounded up the stairs and spilled into the room at that exact moment. There were a dozen or so darkbringers, who all shielded their eyes against the light in the room.

"Not you again!" Billu glared at the new Black Mamba.

"He was the one who came up with the plan to lure you here."

The new Black Mamba shrugged and tilted his hat like he'd received a compliment. "Guilty as charged." He stood up and stretched, arching his back like a cat.

"Time to go," Zeran whispered next to me, but I was already opening a gateway.

"You know what we call it on the rare occasion when we get to feed to our hearts' content?" The new Black Mamba opened the window, and a dozen fireflies careened into the room. "No clue?" he said when we didn't answer. "It's called bloodlust, because once we start, it's nearly impossible to stop."

"Nice to know, but we have to bounce." Three fireflies moved in front of my gateway and quickly transformed into their natural state. The rest of the adze changed and surrounded us.

"Whew, we're going to feast today," the new Black Mamba said.

Zeran cracked his knuckles. "I guess you want to do this the hard way."

The window exploded behind the new Black Mamba. Glass sprayed everywhere. One of the darkbringer recruits threw up a shield just in time to protect us from the shards, which fell harmlessly at our feet.

Two adult darkbringers stood in front of the shattered

window. My heart raced. I would never forget the face of the man who had chased my friends and me across the Dark. The man who looked like an older version of his sons: Commander Rovey.

"Father?" Zeran said in shock.

"Mother?" Billu said as he stared, wide-eyed, at the woman.

Neither of their parents answered. The woman held up her hand, and all the adze fell to their knees like they were locked in invisible chains.

Commander Rovey glared at me before he turned on Black Mamba, who was struggling without success to free himself. In a voice as icy as Antarctica, Commander Rovey said, "Give me one reason why I should spare your miserable lives."

TWENTY-ONE

THE UNEXPECTED

OSHUN'S SECOND RULE was *expect the unexpected.* I never in a million years thought that Commander Rovey would show up here—let alone come with Zeran and Billu's mom. The two stood side by side in front of the broken window. They both wore all black, like spies straight out of an action movie. Zeran and Billu had their dad's cobalt-blue skin and black hair, and they had their mom's horns, only hers were much larger and sloped in an elegant arch away from her face.

Commander Rovey had dark circles underneath his eyes, and his cheeks were sunken. He almost looked remorseful, but I couldn't forget that he locked Zeran in a cage as punishment for joining the Resistance.

"That's our mother," Zeran whispered to me. "Sidda Rovey."

"This little family reunion is all touching and whatnot," the new Black Mamba said as his shoulders twitched. With his arms still pinned to his sides, he rockily climbed to his feet. "But we have a deal with the Lord of Shadows, and y'all breaking it."

Sidda's hold on the other adze was slipping. More of them started to rise from the floor. She and the commander circled around the adze, so their backs were to us. "I don't work for the Lord of Shadows."

Black Mamba licked his lips. "Well, then, that makes you fair game."

"If you're going to do something, *guardian*," Commander Rovey grumbled, "do it now."

I was already *doing* something. My gateway roared to life. "Let's go!" I waved for the darkbringer recruits to follow me, but they hesitated.

"Why should we trust you?" one of them asked. "You're our sworn enemy."

"You can trust me, or you can become someone's else dinner," I said.

Billu shrugged. "She's got a point."

Sidda broke off from holding back the adze and turned to the recruits. "Come, children. There's no time to waste."

Zeran headed into the gateway with his brother,

followed by the other recruits. Then Sidda disappeared down the bridge of god symbols behind them. That left Commander Rovey and me versus a bunch of adze closing in around us. The gateway was already collapsing on this end.

"After you," I insisted.

Commander Rovey wrinkled his nose as we backed into the gateway. "I still don't like you, *godling*."

The adze pushed each other to reach us, but the gateway closed just in time. "Funny, I was thinking the same thing, *Commander*."

A few minutes later, we were back in the warehouse where Zeran and I had left the two darkbringers tied up. It was dark inside, and one of the darkbringer recruits conjured little globes of light that floated above our heads.

Everyone was talking at once. Sidda was doing her best to reassure the recruits that they would be okay, while Billu was recounting how they ended up in Black Mamba's dungeon. Commander Rovey had pulled Zeran aside.

"I know that I don't deserve your forgiveness, but I am sorry all the same," Commander Rovey said. When Zeran only stared at him, unblinking, he added, "I only wanted to keep you from making a mistake. That Resistance you were so eager to join . . . they are no more than gnats for our lord to swat."

"I'm not going back," Zeran said defiantly. "And he's not my lord; he's yours. I'll take my chances in the human world."

"None of us are going back with you." Sidda crossed her arms as she glared at Commander Rovey. "You can stand by and die for the Lord of Shadows, but I will not condemn Zeran and Billu to the same fate."

Commander Rovey cut his eyes at me. "The celestials won't be able to stop him. He'll kill them all, including your father."

I wanted to dismiss the commander's words, but I'd felt the Lord of Shadows' powers firsthand. Still, everyone had a weakness—even him. The celestials would find his weakness, and if not them, then I would. "They'll find a way."

"Do you think the adze are the only ones who have pledged their loyalty to the Lord of Shadows?" Commander Rovey snapped. "The elokos, chupacabras, bogeymen, yetis, and werehyenas . . . they're all on his side."

Eleni had been right about Captain Nulan recruiting in the human world. This was a nightmare come true. Some of the most vicious magical creatures had chosen to join forces with the Lord of Shadows. That still didn't explain why Nulan had let herself get caught. She was smarter than that, and that worried me. "Maybe the odds are against us, but we won't give up."

Zeran put his hands on his hips. "You can convince the Resistance to work with the celestials."

Commander Rovey's top lip curled into an ugly sneer. "What makes you think they'll listen to me?"

Sidda crossed her arms. "Make them listen."

"You're asking me to betray everything I believe in," said Commander Rovey.

"No." Sidda shook her head. "I'm asking you to help make sure there's a future for not only our children but all children."

Zeran pressed his mouth into a tight line to hide his emotions while Billu practically leaned on his tippy toes, waiting for their father's answer. "I'll do it," Commander Rovey spat out as if he had dirt on his tongue. "But I make no promises."

Billu released a shaky breath, but Zeran only stared at his father. Commander Rovey said nothing more as he turned to leave.

"How are you going to find the Resistance?" Sidda asked.

Commander Rovey glanced over his shoulder, taking one last look at his family. "I have my sources."

Once Commander Rovey had left, I opened a gateway back home. Sidda, Billu, and the darkbringer recruits reluctantly followed Zeran and me across the bridge of god symbols. "It'll be okay," I told them. "You'll be safe with us."

Soon we poured out on the sidewalk in front of my house. It was early evening, and it was already dark out. Two familiar swirling blue lights rushed at us. A moment later, Miss Ida and Miss Lucille had taken human forms. Sparks of their godling magic danced on their skin as they held up their hands, preparing to strike.

"Stop!" I shouted as I stepped forward. "They're with me."

Miss Ida and Miss Lucille exchanged a glance, but they lowered their hands. "What have you gotten yourself into now, Maya?" Miss Ida demanded.

Zeran cleared his throat. "To be fair, Miss Ida, she was helping me."

"Maya Janine Abeola!" Mama said as she stepped out of the house with Eleni on her heels. "You were supposed to be resting . . ." She abruptly stopped when she saw the darkbringers, but even they couldn't keep her from scolding me. "You went back to the *Dark*? Of all the irresponsible things to do . . ."

"No, Mama," I said quickly. "Zeran and I went to the bayou to rescue his brother and the other recruits from an adze named Black Mamba." I gestured at Sidda. "This is Zeran's mom, Sidda, by the way. She showed up after I put the first Black Mamba into a deep sleep, and the caretaker became the new Black Mamba."

Sidda, who had been quiet until now, spoke up. "For what it's worth, I'm grateful that your daughter helped save my son." Billu leaned against his mom's side, and she wrapped her arm around his shoulders. Zeran stood nearby with a big grin on his face. "I finally have both my boys back."

Mama relaxed her shoulders and smiled at Sidda.

"You're safe here. As far as I know, there's no adze named Black Mamba in our neighborhood."

Sidda seemed to relax too. "I should hope not."

"I will inform the celestials of your arrival," Miss Ida said. "I'm sure they'll have questions."

Sidda nodded. "I will answer what I can."

"Speaking of the celestials," I said. "Tell them that the Lord of Shadows has recruited the adze and several other magical creatures to his side."

"We know, Maya," Miss Ida admitted. "We've been monitoring the situation, but there isn't much we can do about it."

Miss Lucille clapped her hands. She was in a better mood than her twin. "Sidda, you and the children can come with me. There is much we have to discuss, and I was just about to make dinner."

"Or we could order pizza?" Zeran suggested.

Billu frowned up at his brother. "What's pizza?"

Zeran slapped him on the back. "You're in for a treat."

"Let me get this straight," Eleni said as I climbed the steps to our house. "There are two people named *Black Mamba*?"

I glanced over my shoulder and peered into the shadows beyond the front porch light. I could have sworn something slithered across the pavement. "It's a long story."

TWENTY-TWO

A CITY IN SHADOWS

THE NEXT MORNING, Eleni and I curled up on the sofa in the living room with the curtains opened. The snow was coming down hard now and covered the sidewalks in fresh heaps. We stared glumly at the taillights on cars as the last of our human neighbors drove away. The streets were empty except for the older godlings on patrol. The godlings in elementary school and their families had left for Azur at the crack of dawn. Yemoja and some of the other celestials were at JMS, still trying to find a way to close the wound in the veil.

Papa and Mama were in the kitchen talking to Sidda. "Some celestials have expressed doubts about you and the recruits," Papa was saying. "It's been suggested that your presence here is an elaborate scheme by the Lord of Shadows to trick us."

"And what do you think, Guardian?" Sidda said, her tone icy. "What could a few darkbringers do to all-powerful beings such as yourself? As I recall, you killed countless people when you made the veil. Surely, we are no match for your kind."

Eleni met my gaze as we waited for Papa to answer. When he did speak, his voice was brittle, and I knew even after all this time, the weight of his mistake was still a burden on him. "My daughter Maya is an excellent judge of character, and she wouldn't have brought you here if she had any doubts about your intentions."

Sidda shifted in her chair, and it scraped against the floor as she stood up. "I never wanted my boys to fight. Who in their right mind would want that? But in our world, there is no choice. If you have skills the Lord of Shadows values, you're recruited into his army. I want no part of that, nor do my boys."

"I can't imagine what that must be like," Mama said, as she and Papa stood too. "Your boys and the other children are safe now."

Sidda frowned as the three of them walked into the den. "Nowhere is safe from the Lord of Shadows."

Papa exchanged a glance with Mama, and a silent

understanding passed between the two. It was like when I knew what Eli or Frankie was thinking before they said it. "There is a school in Azur that the Lord of Shadows cannot penetrate," Papa explained. "Obatala made it after the first war. In a sense, it exists in Azur, but it is also separate from Azur. The younger godlings are going there. Your sons and the other darkbringer children can join them."

Sidda shifted on her heels, and her great horns cast a shadow across the wall that made her look even taller. "How many kids can one school hold?"

"This school expands as more people arrive," Papa told her. "It's quite resourceful."

"What about the rest of the world?" Mama asked. "Has a decision been made?"

"Yemoja has convinced the human leaders of the threat, and we're relocating as many people as possible to a suitable planet with similar conditions," Papa said as he and Mama walked with Sidda to the door. "We cannot simply take humans away unless they are willing to leave. Even we have limits imposed by the universe and rules we must follow." Papa stopped cold, his eyes going blank for a split second. "The Lord of Shadows has broken through the first perimeter around the library. Yemoja and the others have fallen back to concentrate their efforts around the second perimeter—*Jackson Middle School.*"

Eleni nudged my arm and whispered, "Maya."

I followed her gaze back to the window. The sky, the trees, and the houses had all turned grayer. Everything was dull. The red curtains at Latesha's living room window, Mr. Mason's blue shutters, the stop sign on the corner, the mural of the three brothers in celebration plastered against the Lees' fence. The small multicolor elephant statue on the Patels' windowsill. The Okekes' bright yellow birdhouse.

I swallowed hard. "It's starting."

Eleni slumped against the couch. "How can anyone stop that?"

For the first time, all I could say was, "I don't know."

The next hour was a frenzy of activity. Papa left to triple-check the third and final perimeter—a veil he'd placed around our neighborhood. Sidda went to the Johnstons' house to get the darkbringer children ready to leave. "Are you girls done packing?" Mama asked as she whisked into the den. "We leave in ten minutes."

"I finished last night," Eleni said.

"And you, Maya?" Mama asked with her hands on her hips.

I sank deeper into the sofa. "I haven't started."

"I'll help you," Eleni said.

"Ten minutes," Mama reiterated, her eyes serious. "Be ready."

Exactly eight minutes later, Eleni and I were rolling our luggage out the front door. Mama said she would meet us at the community center after making a few urgent calls. The metal detector that opened to the gods' realm was a multi-locational gateway that could also take us to Azur.

Miss Ida and Miss Lucille were already outside with Zeran, Billu, their mom, and the other darkbringer children. Each recruit, all nine of them, counting Billu, had duffel bags across their shoulders. When Lucille caught me looking, she said, "We know a good tailor or two."

"Can I walk with Maya and Eleni?" Zeran asked his mom. "I'll meet you once we get to Azur."

Sidda was busy rounding up the other children, who had started to throw snowballs at each other. "Yes, but try to stay out of trouble, Z."

"Z," Eleni mouthed as she looked at Zeran. "Like Dr. Z from the Oya comic books?"

I smirked at Zeran. "Exactly like Dr. Z, diabolical to the end."

Zeran rolled his eyes as we set off to meet up with Eli and Frankie. "I am not diabolical nor am I a scientist bent on world domination."

I winked at him. "Could have fooled me, *Z*."

Zeran only groaned as his cheeks flushed the slightest pink.

When we walked to Eli's house, his auntie was in the kitchen packing food. "What has this world come to? Ghosts? Evil overlords? Your grandmother is a celestial.

You're godlings. On my side of the family, we're just plain folk. Do you hear that, Eli and Jayla? We're plain folk. We aren't messing around with no evil overlords."

Auntie Bae was taking the whole celestials, godlings, and overlord thing better than I'd thought she would.

Jayla bounced down the stairs with an armful of toys. Eli screamed after her, "You're supposed to pack *useful* things."

One of Jayla's dolls turned its head. "We're useful *and* quite fashionable."

This was new. Even Jayla had come into her godling powers.

"He's wearing mismatched socks," said another doll. "Somebody call the fashion police."

"I heard that!" Eli shouted at the top of the stairs.

Jayla giggled as she put the dolls in her luggage.

With Eli in tow, we headed for Frankie's. When we reached her house, her moms were arguing over whether they should take one or two microscopes to Azur in addition to the one that Frankie had already packed.

"We need three," Dee said as she delicately placed glass beakers into a foam case. "It's a new world, one built in the clouds. There are bound to be plenty of new bacteria to discover. Can you imagine?"

"That and the ability to study various forms of magic up close," Pam said. "I wonder if it's measurable like sound waves or the speed of light. That would be something."

"Um, is Frankie here?" I asked, interrupting their conversation.

"You just missed her." Dee shoved a telescope into a case. "She left for Azur about an hour ago. Apparently, there's a library that contains the history of the universe, and she wanted to visit it."

"Oh," I said quietly. There was only one reason why Frankie could have gone to the library. She wanted to find out about the Azurians in the photo of her orisha mom at the farmers' market. From the sound of it, she hadn't told her moms her reason for wanting to go early.

When we left Frankie's house headed for the community center, Eleni said, sadly, "I hope she finds something."

"She will—believe that!" Eli said confidently. "This is Frankie we're talking about, as in Frankie, the Frankiefier, the Frankster, the Frankiestein, the—"

"We get the point," Zeran said, cutting him off.

I was on edge when we arrived at the community center. The last of the younger godlings and their noncelestial parents filed through the metal detector and disappeared.

Nana was up ahead, reassuring people that everything would be okay. She hugged Jayla tightly with tears in her eyes. "Take care of your sister," she said to Eli. "And try to stay out of trouble."

What was it with the adults and thinking we would get into trouble?

"I will, Nana," he said as she pulled him into an embrace too.

All around us, godlings were saying goodbye to their celestial family members. Winston, Tay, and Candace had already found each other and were loudly proclaiming that they should be allowed to stay behind to help. "What a waste of talent," Winston fumed. "I almost single-handedly stopped the Lord of Shadows myself. Everyone knows it."

Papa was waiting for us by the metal detector. He stood tall, his shoulders proud, but his eyes were sad. Eleni and I stayed back while our friends went through the gateway. "I'm going to miss you so much," Papa said, dropping to one knee.

Neither of us complained about him not coming to Azur. We knew it was useless. His job was here. He would always be the guardian of the veil as long as it stood, always be tasked with helping to protect the world. I felt that drive too, to protect those who couldn't defend themselves. I understood his decision and that he had responsibilities, but that didn't make this any easier.

"We're going to miss you too, Papa," Eleni said as she threw herself into his arms.

Papa kissed the top of her head. "Take care of each other, baby girl."

"We will," Eleni said through her sobs.

Papa turned to me. "Maya, don't do anything else risky, okay?"

I bit my bottom lip. "I'll do my best."

Papa quirked an eyebrow. "You'll do better than your best."

"Yes, Papa," I said, hugging him. I tried hard not to cry and utterly failed.

Papa said his goodbyes to Mama and whispered something in her ear. Eleni and I turned away. My sister looked miserable, and I was sure I did too. Moments later, the three of us entered the gateway to Azur, leaving Papa behind. I wiped away my tears. I would be brave; I was still a guardian in training and would do my part to keep my family safe.

The whole trip took only a few minutes, and we arrived in the city in the clouds. "Those with children under sixteen, please proceed to Arch A," an Azurian floating above our heads said, directing the crowd. He was reptilian, with golden scales and wings attached to his arms like a bat. His hair stood straight up and was a rainbow of colors. "Godlings assigned to peacekeeper duties, please proceed to Arch B. All other visitors, please proceed to Arch C for a provisional assignment." He repeated the announcement as godlings and their human families spread out across the courtyard.

The arches stood on the north side of the plaza. Arch A

was filled with light that pulsed each time someone passed underneath it. Arch B was made of twisted black vines that crawled between the feet of the older godlings who'd signed up for peacekeeper duty. They would help protect Azur in case the celestials failed in our neighborhood. Arch C—the provisional assignment gate—was the least active. A group of elokos chattered nonstop as they passed through a ring of flames.

"Those guys again." Eli slapped his forehead. "They better not have a taste for human flesh." He was still holding a grudge after another group of elokos had tried to eat us in Daniel Boone National Forest this past summer.

Miss Ida and Miss Lucille led Sidda and the darkbringer children to Arch A, but the twins stopped short of going inside. This was by far the busiest gate, as godlings from our neighborhood stepped through the yellow light. Tisha, Naomi, Maurice, August, RayShawn, Winston, Candace, Tay. All the godlings from Jackson Middle.

Mama stared at the fluffy clouds beneath her feet. "I think I'm going to be sick—that is if I don't fall to my death first."

Pam scooped up a sample of a cloud in a beaker. "I can't wait to get this under my microscope."

"We'll set up a full lab at the school," Dee said, almost squealing with excitement. "Think of the scientific discoveries just waiting to be made."

"Mama, would it be okay if we go to the library?" I asked. "Frankie's there."

"Yes, but meet us at the school at lunchtime," Mama said. "We need to make sure that everyone's accounted for."

"Yes, ma'am," I said as we set off.

Eleni, Zeran, Eli, and I pushed our way through the crowd of godlings taking in Azur for the first time. They were trying the ice cream that tastes like anything your heart desires, the evaporating cotton candy, the pickled donuts (which weren't as bad as they sounded), and other delicacies. The bustling scene was so different from our neighborhood, which had been a ghost town when we left, but it gave me hope. Maybe things would be okay. Maybe the Lord of Shadows and his minions would make a mistake.

We asked for directions to the library and started on our way, but not before getting Zeran an ice cream cone. "This tastes exactly like my mother's kimban pie," he said, loudly smacking his lips.

"What is kimban?" Eli asked, curious.

"It's a fruit," Zeran said. "It's sour and sweet at the same time . . . like Lemonheads."

"I wouldn't mind some Lemonheads right now," Eli said.

We were halfway to the library when I got a prickly sensation down my back. Some of the godlings stopped in our path and pointed at the sky. The Azurians clutched their young children and hurried away. Eleni gasped next to me at the same time I saw it. A dark cloud rolled in like a silent storm. Lightning struck, followed by thunder that shook the ground.

Zeran flexed his fingers. "I don't think that's normal."

That was definitely *not* normal. The weather was always perfect here.

The Azurian directing people shouted, "Stay calm and proceed to your arch immediately. Hurry!"

An alarm blasted over a loudspeaker as the dark cloud completely blocked the sun.

"It's the prisoners!" someone screamed. "They've escaped from Alsar."

TWENTY-THREE

AMBUSH

THE SIREN BLASTED again and echoed in the market. The cloud was spreading as lightning cut across the sky. The Azurians quickly fled, some taking flight, some disappearing into thin air, some barricading themselves inside sweetshops. The last of the godlings and their families ran for the arches. "Wasn't Alsar where Sky Father took Captain Nulan?" I asked as the streets emptied.

"Yes," Eleni said, her voice small. "It houses the most dangerous magical criminals in the entirety of the universe."

"Just what we need, the most dangerous criminals in the universe free," Eli said.

I frowned, thinking back to when we captured Nulan. "She tricked us," I said, putting it together. "Captain Nulan wanted to go to Alsar. What better place to recruit than a prison full of people who hate the celestials' rules?"

Zeran stared up at the cloud getting closer. "She's not one of the Lord of Shadows' favorite cronies for nothing."

An Azurian in a white uniform stepped in our path. Her skin was gray and smooth in a way that blended in with the background behind her. She didn't have hair or eyebrows—or eyelids, for that matter. Zigzag lines, almost like tattoos, covered her bald head. I blinked once, twice, then a third time. I was having a hard time focusing on her face. "Didn't you hear the sirens?" she asked. "You're not supposed to be here."

I swallowed my nerves. "Is Tyana Nulan free? Did she release the other prisoners?"

"Come with me," the woman insisted, gesturing for us to follow her. She must have seen our hesitation. Hello, hadn't she heard of *stranger danger*? You don't just leave with some random person. That could lead to nothing but trouble. "I am a peacekeeper, and we're getting everyone to safety until the criminals can be apprehended."

More peacekeepers flooded the streets. They helped the Azurians and godlings who were clamoring to get to the arches. "We have to go to the library to get our friend first," I said, rushing my words.

"I will accompany you," the peacekeeper said sharply, then she turned without another word.

By the time we reached the musical cobblestones outside

the library, it wasn't my imagination that each step sounded like a note of doom that grew increasingly bleaker. It reminded me of a piano so far out of tune that it could be mistaken for nails on a chalkboard. Gargoyles perched on the slanted roof of the library were flapping their wings against the wind.

The hinges creaked as the peacekeeper pushed open the double doors. We stepped into the lobby beneath high ceilings decorated in crystals hanging from strings. The walls were lined with portraits, starting with Alvarra "Tiny" Teek, the current head librarian, according to the metal plaque. There had to be hundreds of portraits arranged in neat rows from the top of the walls to the bottom, each of a past head librarian.

Eli fanned his hand in front of his face. "It smells like a ten-day-old fart in here."

"How would you know what a ten-day-old fart smells like?" I asked, narrowing my eyes at him. He really could be ridiculous sometimes.

He winked at me. "Trust me, I know."

Eleni inhaled deeply as she took in the sight of the library. "That's the smell of well-worn books that have stood the test of time."

We stopped in front of the empty check-out desk. Three long hallways branched out from the lobby, each shrouded in shadows. In the back of the library, a staircase spiraled up to a second-floor balcony. It was so quiet that we could hear our footsteps echoing. The thought crossed my mind that Frankie might have left with the rest of the people who were evacuating, but we had to be sure.

"Frankie could be anywhere," I said. "This place is huge."

The doors to the library slammed shut behind us, and the peacekeeper stood in front of them, tapping one of her heels. She wore an ugly smile, and for the first time, I realized that I'd seen her somewhere before. "The four of you are so pathetic. Two want-to-be guardians, a boy who relies on ghosts to fight his battles, and the traitor." Her voice dropped into a mocking tone. "Looking for the girl with the dead mother, are you?"

That was cold. I might have been wrong, but I got the distinct feeling that this peacekeeper had a bone to pick with us. "Who are you?"

"I am called Butcher," she spat. "I heard you were looking for my friends and me."

"Butcher," Eleni spluttered. "That's . . . um, quite a name you have there."

"You're about to find out how I earned it," Butcher said proudly.

I wracked my brain, trying to figure out her connection to us. The more I stared at her, the harder it became to concentrate on her face, like she was being erased from my memory in real time. Then I thought about the picture of Frankie's mom. The woman with the blurry face in the background—*it was her.*

The missing piece snapped in place. I remembered the suspicious squirrel on our walk home from school. "Where's Frankie?" I demanded, my voice trembling. I wouldn't let myself fear the worst.

Butcher smiled, and it was full of spite and mischief. "You four will fetch a fair reward from the Lord of Shadows. Better than the one I got for helping break Tyana Nulan and the others out of prison."

Her words cut deep. Everything was falling apart. The Lord of Shadows had yet another ally. Captain Nulan was free, along with all the prisoners from Alsar. And here was another crony looking to seed chaos with no regard for anyone else. She didn't have to come out and say what happened to Frankie's mom. She wasn't called Butcher for nothing.

Eli cracked his knuckles, and an icy breeze swept through the room. Shadows peeled away from the portraits on the walls and settled into the ghosts of the past head librarians.

"What is happening in my library?" one of them said.

"Is that dust on my portrait?" said another. "How untidy."

"I need you to focus," Eli told them, then he turned back to Butcher. "*Where. Is. Frankie?*"

Butcher wagged her finger. "That's for me to know and you to find out." Two figures emerged from the shadows. The man at the top of the spiraling staircase was twice the size of a pro wrestler, with bulging biceps and sharp spikes along his forearms. The second man appeared in the mouth of the hallway in front of us. He had translucent skin, puckered fish lips, and four tentacles instead of arms and legs. These were the other two Azurians in the photo with Frankie's mom. "Meet my friend Spike," Butcher said, looking up at the man on the balcony, then she turned to the one with the tentacles. "And Crusher."

"Did you clowns get your names from the back of a cereal box or what?" Eli said as his ghosts closed ranks. "So unoriginal."

Butcher smiled again, revealing sharp, pointed teeth that hadn't been there moments ago. Conveniently, she also had grown claws. Eleni let out a little gasp beside me, and I swallowed hard. Zeran tugged at his sleeves. Then he seemed to realize that he'd lost his prods when we went up against the adze in the bayou. Instead, he tried to make one of his animations. The chairs and tables and photos in the lobby shook, but they resisted his pull.

The attack came at once. Spike leaped over the balcony and landed in a crouch. Then he was on the move, headed straight for Eli and Zeran. Crusher whipped out one of his tentacles and grabbed my ankle. He squeezed so hard that it felt as if my bone would snap in two. I hit the floor, but not before I swung my staff and connected with my target. Crusher yelped and fell back.

"Maya, are you okay?" Eleni screamed as she ran to my side.

"I think my ankle's broken," I said through gritted teeth.

Eli's ghosts fought off Spike, but the big Azurian kept slipping through their grasps. Zeran was doing combat with Butcher while Crusher's tentacles wrapped around Eleni, pinning her arms and wings to her sides. I tried to get to my feet again, but my ankle had swollen to the size of a grapefruit. "Let my sister go!" I yelled.

"Stop!" Eleni commanded, winded. Fairy dust floated in the air around her, and I had a sudden feeling of wanting to stay completely still. "You will never hurt anyone else again."

Her fairy dust settled on Crusher's tentacles and disappeared. He gritted his teeth like he was trying to fight her magic, but in the end, he slid to the floor and drew his knees to his chest. Eleni slumped against me, exhausted.

Butcher had Zeran on his knees, with her claws to his throat. "I've had enough of this foolishness," she said. "It's time to end this."

She grunted as something—not something, *someone*—knocked her to the floor. It had to be Eli in ghost mode. Butcher hissed and let loose a purple mist.

"Get them off," Eli screamed as he became visible again. The purple mist had settled on him and transformed into spiders. His ghosts faded one by one.

"Oh dear," said a stately head librarian wearing a top hat. He was the last ghost to disappear.

"They're not real, Eli," Zeran yelled. "It's a trick."

Butcher laughed. "Oh, they're very real."

Mama used peppermint spray to keep spiders out of the house. I stood up, hopping on one foot, and pointed the staff at Eli. A second later, I caught a whiff of peppermint in the air, and the spiders scattered.

Wait, where was Spike? I turned, but not fast enough. Spike lifted me into the air with one massive hand, and my staff slipped out of my grasp. "I find you to be very annoying, godling," he growled. "Time to put you out of your misery."

"I think not," I said, driving my knee into his belly.

Spike laughed. "You're a funny little one, aren't you?"

"Hey, Spike," Eleni said with my staff reared back. "You should wear better shoes."

I cocked my head to the side, and Spike frowned right before Eleni slammed the staff on top of his foot. He dropped me. Then he lunged at Eleni. She pivoted low, spun, and hit him with the staff twice. That only made him growl louder.

Air suddenly whooshed into the room, and a peacekeeper with tufts of hair covering his face stood, half-crouched.

His yellow eyes landed on the scene. It was Charlie, the kishi who knew Frankie's mom. I never thought I would be so happy to see him again. Soon the lobby was swarming with peacekeepers, and they quickly apprehended Crusher and Spike.

Somewhere glass shattered, and Zeran shouted, "She's getting away."

I looked in time to see Butcher climb out of a window and disappear.

Eli stopped checking himself for spiders and glared at Charlie. "Oh, now you show up after ignoring Frankie for weeks."

"I haven't been ignoring her." Charlie cackled, baring his very sharp teeth. "I've been busy keeping the peace." He looked around. "Where is she?"

"We're about to find out," I said, turning on Spike and Crusher, who the other peacekeepers had lassoed together. "Where is Frankie?"

Spike spat on the floor. "Eat dirt, little godling."

I shoved my staff against his chest. "So we're going to do this the hard way, okay then."

"Hold on, Sister," Eleni said, then she addressed Crusher: "You'll tell us."

"Tell them nothing!" Spike barked.

But Crusher's eyes were still glazed over from fairy magic. "Tyana Nulan took her," he said in a robotic voice.

I cursed under my breath—and I was glad Mama wasn't here to wash my mouth out with soap. "Where?"

Crusher shrugged with a sleepy look. "I don't know."

Charlie spun around so the human side of his head faced us. His human cheek was slightly less hairy than his hyena side, but not by much. Instead of a growl, his voice was rough around the edges. "I want to help you get Frankie back, but my duties must come first. If I don't track down Butcher, she'll destroy everyone who has the misfortune to be in her path."

There could only be one reason Nulan had taken Frankie: she wanted us to come after her. But it didn't matter if it was a trap. I had to rescue my friend.

TWENTY-FOUR

A MENACE

ELI MOCKINGLY WAVED at Crusher and Spike as the peacekeepers dragged them away. Still dazed with fairy magic, Crusher smiled and waved back with all four of his tentacles. Spike growled and twisted in his bonds, but the peacekeepers held on tight to him.

"Phew," Eli said once they were gone. "Those two would be all right if they weren't the absolute worst ever." He cleared his throat, his face turning serious. "How are we going to find Frankie, and when do we leave?"

"Why would Captain Nulan take Frankie?" Zeran asked.

"Nulan has never been the subtle type." I bit my lip. "She had a reason."

"Maybe it's to distract us from something else," Eleni

suggested. "She freed the prisoners from Alsar, so we can assume they'll use the gateway to mount a surprise attack on the celestials."

"The gateway between Azur and earth closed as soon as the first sirens went off," said a ghost who had suddenly appeared in a corner with his nose in a book. He had huge black eyes behind thick glasses and wore frilly lace and long polka-dot socks. "It's a precaution."

"What are you doing still here?" Eli said. "I didn't call you back."

"I'm Rana Kane, the 112th head librarian of the greatest library in the entire universe, and I live here," the ghost said, not bothering to look up from his book. "For what it's worth, the young guardian is right. Some of the prisoners from Alsar are on their way to earth, traveling the old-fashioned way. I overheard those nasty fellows talking about it before you arrived."

"What's the old-fashioned way?" Eleni asked.

"By vehicles of some sort." Rana Kane shrugged. "Of course, in my heyday, we favored horse-drawn carriages." He turned a page in his book. "In any case, you should leave that business to the adults. All children should report to the school, where you'll find safety and shelter."

As if on cue, a loud explosion outside rocked the library. The crystals hanging from the ceiling knocked into each other, and several head librarians' portraits crashed to the floor. We could hear shouting, cackling, and hissing all at once, and lightning struck the ground outside of the window. The peacekeepers had their hands full.

Papa said the Lord of Shadows had never been able to attack the school. I wondered how the orishas had protected it. "Why is the school the safest place?"

"No adults can enter the school unless they are accompanied by a child who received an invitation," Rana Kane said, finally looking up from his book. "Though all children are free to come and go, whether or not they have an invitation."

"Wait, are you saying any kid can get to the school?" Eli asked, his eyebrows pinched into a deep frown. "*Any kid?*"

"Of course," Rana Kane said dismissively. "That's the point—Sky Father built the school to protect all children."

The lobby in the library went so quiet that you could hear a feather drop. Eleni gasped and covered her mouth. Zeran looked miserable, and Eli had turned a ghastly color. My stomach churned as I clutched my staff tighter.

I'd never thought about why the Lord of Shadows had recruited children into his army, but I should've realized that he had a reason. He'd wanted to hurt the celestials, and what better way than through their children? Rule number four: *never underestimate your opponent.*

"Jayla's at that school," Eli said, his voice going hoarse.

"So is Billu," Zeran mumbled.

"And my mom," I whispered.

Rana Kane frowned. "I get the feeling that I'm missing something."

"What are we going to do?" Eleni asked, crossing her arms.

I stared at my friends' faces—the anguish, the fear, the determination. We couldn't let ourselves fall apart. "We divide and conquer. I'll look for Frankie. Zeran and Eli, go to the school to make sure everyone's okay. Eleni—"

"I'll warn Papa and the other celestials about the prisoners from Alsar," she finished. "I can open a gateway and beat them there."

"Right," I said, uneasy. I didn't like the idea of separating, but the way I saw it, we didn't have a choice. "We'll meet at the school in one hour."

"One hour," Eli said, then he and Zeran pushed through the library doors and stepped into a cloud of fog.

Eleni hugged me before she opened a gateway. "Be safe, Sister."

"You too," I said before she disappeared. "One hour."

I tightened my grasp on my staff and directed my magic to find Captain Nulan. If I wanted to rescue Frankie, I'd have to go through her. When I was in the Dark, I could sense Papa. Maybe this would work too. I closed my eyes, and I could see glimpses of Nulan. Her wicked smile, the arch of her eyebrow, the flutter of her wings, the glimmer of her slim knives. I opened my eyes, my heart beating fast, just as the gateway opened. "Here I go."

I crossed the bridge of spinning god symbols, following an echo of Nulan that manifested itself like a ghost. When I exited at the other end, I landed on a barren planet of rocks, sand, and dead trees. There was no one in sight—no buildings, no structures of any kind. I didn't understand. Nulan wasn't here. I turned in a circle, confused, until I saw a knife lodged in a tree a few feet away. Not just any knife—one of Nulan's slender blades. It was a message, that much was for sure. *Catch me if you're quick enough.*

"Find Frankie," I whispered as I cut the staff through the air, and another gateway opened.

This time, I landed on a world blanketed in fog and found another slender blade. Then I opened a third, fourth, and fifth gateway, growing more desperate. I was breathing hard, exhausted from the effort. Somehow Nulan was hiding Frankie and herself from my gateways while leaving a trail for me to follow. I wiped the sweat from my forehead and leaned against my staff. Without the ability to make a gateway, it must've taken months for Nulan to plant these false leads, which meant that she'd been in the human world a long time before we encountered her at the city dump. *But why?*

I swallowed hard and took a deep breath. I was never going to find Nulan at this rate. Papa taught me two ways to travel long distances quickly. One was building a gateway between two points, aka a bridge. That was faster than any nonmagical form of transportation, but there was an even quicker way. Papa rarely made gateways; he opened portals by bending space itself. He'd warned me that it was more dangerous to bend the space between two points if you didn't know what you were doing. I'd never tried. I didn't think I was ready, but I didn't see another way to get to Nulan faster.

I squeezed the staff, and the symbols started to glow brighter. Instinctively, I realized that to bend space, I must perceive it. I had to reach out and touch it. The symbols peeled off the staff and scattered around me. A lion leaped across my path. A tree bearing golden fruit sprouted from the ground. A sun with shimmering rays moved across the sky. The symbol for pi floated at eye level toward me, pulsing with golden light. Not a real pie, but the mathematical pi, 3.14 and the string of numbers that followed it. Thousands of symbols danced around me, but they didn't keep their shapes for long. They blurred around the edges and then stretched out into long golden threads.

When I touched one of the threads, it vibrated against my fingertips. I thought I understood—the threads connected everything in the universe. I concentrated on finding Nulan again, and one of the threads pulsed brighter while the rest became dim. Her petty tricks didn't fool the portal.

A fuzzy image appeared in front of me. Nulan stood under a starry night, and Frankie lay in a ball at her feet.

"I should be on the front line," Nulan murmured angrily to herself. "This is . . ."

I snatched the thread, and I was there with her.

". . . beneath me." Her words trailed off, and her lips curled into a vicious smile. "I should've realized that you'd be the one to catch up with me. My niece is too weak. She always has been, but no matter, you'll do just fine."

I bit my lip. I wouldn't let Nulan bait me. Eleni was far from weak. She was smart, strong, and caring. She was everything I could ever wish for in a sister. "This ends here."

Nulan grimaced as she looked up at the empty pocket of the sky where stars had been only a moment ago. Had I done that when I opened the portal? "You are a menace, just like your father."

"You want to talk about being *a menace*?" I said, my blood boiling with anger. "You serve a person who has no regard for life, not even for the darkbringers who believe in him. He sends children to fight his battles. Do you think when the veil finally comes down, he'll ever stop? He'll never be satisfied."

"Enough of this talk!" Captain Nulan's eyes darkened as gold and silver fairy magic spread around her.

I threw up a shield of god symbols, but not before the fairy dust hit me. I staggered back, dazed and more than a little confused. I tried to brush it off my clothes, but my arms fell slack at my sides.

"As I told you before, my lord *needs* you alive," Nulan said.

I hadn't seen this coming. Nulan was an aziza, and like Eleni, she could use her magic to control others. This was her plan all along—*how could I let her trick me?* I wanted to ask why the Lord of Shadows needed me, but I thought I already knew the answer. Oshun was right. He wouldn't stop once he had control of earth. Not when he could travel the entirety of the universe, across multiple worlds in moments . . . with a little help.

"Maya Janine Abeola," Captain Nulan said. I hated the sound of my name coming from her. I hated what she was about to do, and I hated that I couldn't stop her. "You will serve the Lord of Shadows faithfully for the rest of your life."

Her magic twisted around my mind like a rope, making me forget why I was here and what I was fighting for. I couldn't serve the Lord of Shadows, but I had to, *didn't I?* It was my duty. No, it was *my privilege.* That wasn't right. He was the bad guy—*wasn't he?* Eleni once said that fairy magic was about suggestions, that someone with a disciplined mind could break free. But Nulan's magic was stronger than anything I had ever felt from Eleni, and it was quickly unraveling my will to resist.

I clenched my teeth as I looked to Frankie, who was still on the ground. Seeing my friend unconscious only fueled my anger. The Lord of Shadows said that I was danger-ous—more dangerous than him. I had destroyed dozens of stars by pulling one thread. I hadn't meant it, but inten-tions and results weren't the same things. I pushed against Nulan's magic so forcefully that my nose started to bleed. But the more I fought, the stronger her magic became. I fell to my knees under the weight of it.

Nulan stood over me. "Tell me, Maya, who do you serve?"

I struggled to talk, my mouth opening and closing. The answer seemed too obvious, so completely clear. I had no doubts. I smiled up at Nulan and proudly said, "I serve the Lord of Shadows." The words sounded all wrong, like they were coming from someone else.

Nulan smiled back at me, victory dancing in her eyes. "You will forget this conversation, and you will pretend to be loyal to your friends until the time comes when our lord calls upon you to act. Do you understand?"

"Yes," I said, my head fuzzy. "I understand."

"We'll be seeing you very soon," Nulan said as she backed away into the darkness.

I closed my eyes. A moment later, I was blinking up at a starless night. Of all the rotten times to get dizzy, this had to be the rottenest. Where was Nulan? The last thing

I remembered was telling her that the Lord of Shadows wouldn't stop once the veil came down.

Frankie groaned next to me. "What happened?"

I reached over and straightened her crooked glasses. "You're safe, but Nulan got away."

I couldn't shake the feeling that I had forgotten something—something that was a matter of life or death.

TWENTY-FIVE

THE INTERGALACTIC SCHOOL FOR THE MAGICALLY GIFTED

As THE LAST of my dizziness faded, I still couldn't shake the feeling that I had forgotten something, but it didn't matter. Frankie was okay except for a few scrapes and bruises. She climbed to her feet and turned in a circle, looking at the gloom around us and the missing stars.

"I was in the library reading through the public records when I saw the woman in the photo with my first mom," Frankie said, blinking back tears. "She was a peacekeeper nicknamed Butcher because most of the magical criminals she tracked down ended up . . ." Frankie drew a single finger across her throat. "You know . . . *dead*."

"We had the misfortune of meeting her and the other two Azurians in the photo—Crusher and Spike," I told her.

"Charlie and the other peacekeepers captured them, but she got away."

"Butcher said that my mom found out that she was secretly working for a big crime boss, so Butcher disposed of her." Frankie swiped hard at the tears on her cheeks. "When this business with the Lord of Shadows is over, I'm going after Butcher."

My heart ached for Frankie. Butcher had to be stopped before she hurt someone else. "I'm going with you," I said quietly. "We have to bring her to justice."

Frankie let out a shaky breath. "Thanks for saving me." She looked around again. "Where's everyone else?"

I cut my staff across the space in front of us, but I could feel the gateway resisting me. I frowned. "We were supposed to meet at the school in Azur, but I can't open a gateway there."

Frankie adjusted her glasses, which had fogged up from her crying. "Oh, that's right." She perked up a little. "I read about the school at the library. It's protected by magic. We can only enter if it lets us."

"So why isn't it letting us?" I asked, remembering how Eli and Zeran had gone ahead to make sure the school was still safe. Was there something wrong?

"While I was at the library, I read that the school didn't exist in one place," Frankie said. "That must be why you can't open a gateway directly there."

"Grand," I said, frustrated.

Frankie shrugged with a goofy look on her face. "Someone once told me that *magic explains the unexplainable.*"

"I did say that, didn't I?" I thought about Shangó's theory that the Lord of Shadows drew his power from dark energy and got an idea. "Do you think that dark energy can exist in bubbles outside of space and time?"

Frankie tilted her head to one side and furrowed her eyebrows. "I suppose it could be possible," she said. "But if you're thinking what I think you're thinking, the hard part would be to get the Lord of Shadows in that bubble."

Maybe it was another dead end, but I couldn't get Shangó's theory out of my head. The celestials couldn't kill the Lord of Shadows. That much was clear. He was too powerful, but if he was weakened enough, he might be able to be contained forever. I groaned in frustration. It was all just so . . . theoretical. It didn't matter anyway. I would be stuck on Azur while the celestials did their *celestial thing*.

I redirected my gateway to open near the arch that led to the school. I wondered if Eleni had gotten back from our neighborhood yet and what news she would bring. "Time to take a little detour."

Frankie gave me a nervous look before we stepped onto the bridge of god symbols. When we exited in the middle of the market in Azur, there was no one left on the streets—not even a peacekeeper. The sky was purple and gray, like a brewing storm, but it wasn't completely dark. All the shops had been closed, and some had disappeared entirely, as if the shopkeepers had carried them off. All that was left were the lingering smells of sugar, butter, cinnamon, and popcorn.

"Maya, the arches," Frankie said at my side. "They're gone."

Rana Kane, the ghost of the 112th librarian, had said the gateway between Azur and earth had closed after the first alarm went off, but he failed to mention that the arches would eventually disappear too. "This is inconvenient."

"If my memory serves me correctly, which I'm sure it does, the school has a physical location in Azur," Frankie said. "We passed it months ago when we visited Sky Father's hut."

A scream pierced the silence of the market, followed by manic laughter. "Oh look, two new mice to play with" came a haunting voice that echoed against the buildings.

I pushed back my fear as a low fog moved through the cobblestones. Electricity sparked on Frankie's palms.

"We have to get to the school," I said, but as soon as I did, my foot caught on something, and I almost tripped. "What the . . . ?"

I stared down in horror at the leg poking from behind an overturned food cart. Frankie and I both stopped cold. I was afraid to look any closer, thinking that the leg might be missing the rest of its body parts, but then it moved. We peered behind the cart, where a woman lay against a wall, cradling a wound across her chest.

"Are you okay?" Frankie asked.

"Do I look okay?" the woman moaned with her eyes still squeezed shut.

I kneeled at her side. "Do you need help getting up?"

"I'd rather stay here." The woman opened her eyes, and they were hollow. When she smiled, she didn't have a tongue or teeth. It was like looking into a tunnel of darkness. "There's much fun left to play."

I jumped back. Okay. Nope. I'd had enough of diabolical villains for the day.

"Let's keep moving," I told Frankie, and thankfully the woman didn't follow us.

We set off again, but this time at a jog, barely missing gaping holes in the cloud beneath our feet. By the time we arrived at the edge of the school grounds, we were half out of breath. The plaque on the gate read: INTERGALACTIC SCHOOL FOR THE MAGICALLY GIFTED. Behind it stood an empty field. No buildings, no trees, no sign that anything or anyone had ever been here.

"I should have thought of this," Frankie lamented. "If the school doesn't really exist in one place. It must have moved when the prisoners attacked Azur."

"Convenient for the school, doubly inconvenient for us," I groaned.

"There has to be a trick to it," Frankie said.

"Rana Kane, the 112th librarian, said the school is always open to children in need, and we're in need."

Something—scratch that, *some things* moved in the fog, creeping closer to us. We had to figure this out and fast. On a hunch, I pushed open the gate. It was heavy but offered no resistance. "I have an idea," I said. "What if we wait for it to come for us?"

Frankie peered at the shadows drawing closer. "What makes you think it will?"

"It's just a . . . *um* . . . theory," I told her as we stepped onto the manicured lawn.

"Two tiny morsels to eat," sang a voice in the fog. "What a tasty little treat."

"They're mine!" shouted another voice.

"Let's play a game," suggested a third.

"Pick their bones clean," sang the first voice. "They look mighty lean."

Frankie gulped hard. "Let's hope you're right about the school coming back."

I slammed the gate behind us, but there was no lock—not that I thought it would help. We backed away, and the fog stopped just short of crossing the gate. It pressed against the wrought iron, rolling over itself like a den of snakes. "You can't hide in there forever," hissed one of the voices.

I almost thought we were in the clear until something

knocked against the gate. It began to creak, and the ground shook beneath our feet.

"We might be in trouble," I murmured.

"*Might be* is an understatement," Frankie said.

Something whooshed behind us, and I crouched and spun around. A single door had appeared in the middle of the empty field with light pouring from it. "Could it be as simple as that?" I asked, staring in disbelief.

"I guess we're going to find out," Frankie said.

We dashed through the door and landed in the grass on the other side. The door disappeared. We were on the lawn about a dozen feet from the school's main building, near a marble statue of a woman holding a plaque that read: WELCOME TO THE INTERGALACTIC SCHOOL FOR THE MAGICALLY GIFTED.

We hadn't had time to process where we were when a window exploded in the building directly in front of us. Dread twisted in my stomach as I saw flashes of godling-blue magic. "The school is under attack," I said as we set off at a sprint.

"So much for being impenetrable," Frankie shouted.

The fighting was in the main building at the center of campus, and when we burst through the door, the scene was unimaginable. Some three dozen ghosts flooded the hall as Eli's archnemesis, Carran, floated above the floor, controlling them. Normally, I wouldn't hate being right, but I wished I were wrong this time. Carran and the other dark-bringers had only been able to attack the school because they were children.

Zeran and Eli were fighting side by side with Winston, Tay, and Candace. They held the front line, battling the ghosts. As Oya would say: *What's the point of having power if you don't use it to make the world a better place?* Begrudgingly, I was glad to see Winston and his cronies . . . *um*, his friends. At their backs, the rest of the godlings, along with Billu and the former recruits, fought the other darkbringers.

My heart pounded against my chest. Where were Mama, Pam, Dee, the other adults, and the younger godlings like Jayla? They had to be okay. I refused to think about the alternative.

"A little help here, Brother," Billu called as his Darkzilla batted back four darkbringers.

Zeran ducked and rolled out of the way of a can that Tisha Thomas had accidentally hurtled too close to his head. She didn't have any defensive magic, so she was taking the battle to the darkbringers the old-fashioned way.

"Oops!" Tisha shouted. "So, Zeran, I was wrong about you. Sorry!"

"Just try not to take my head off," he said, dashing to his brother's side.

Frankie and I joined the fight. "About time you showed up," Winston said, casting me a crooked grin. "Thought we would have to save the day again."

I knocked back two darkbringers with my staff. "We couldn't let you have all the fun."

"Where's Eleni?" I called out to Zeran as his animation formed next to Darkzilla. It was another collection of objects from the room, and it was massive.

"Haven't seen her," he answered over the roar of the fight. "You're the first to get here."

I staggered, barely raising my staff in time to block a blow. Eleni wasn't back. *She wasn't back.* I glanced around quickly, looking for a clock. It had been over two hours since we'd parted ways at the library. My sister was always punctual. Always. If she wasn't back, something had gone wrong.

TWENTY-SIX

WE NEED A RIDE

I SWUNG MY STAFF and sent god symbols flying at the darkbringers closest to me. Zeran's and Billu's animations were inflicting their fair share of damage on another group of darkbringers. Even Winston, Tay, and Candace had knocked several darkbringers out cold. Every time we defeated a darkbringer, the other godlings dragged them to the corner of the main hall where Frankie had created a forcefield to hold them.

Eli stood off against Carran with the ghost army lined up between them. The ghosts were frozen in place. "You're the last darkbringer left," Eli said. "You should give up while you still can."

Carran grimaced as she looked around the hall. The rest of the darkbringers had been neutralized, but she cracked her knuckles. "I have no intention of giving up, ghost boy. I will not be bested by the likes of you."

"You know the thing about ghosts," Eli said, smiling. "They'll help if you ask nicely. But you keep trying to bend them to your will. They don't like that."

"Ghosts are meant to be tamed," Carran countered. "They aren't alive, nor do they need to be asked nicely."

Carran's blue skin had gone a shade paler. Her hands were balled into fists, and she was shaking. Eli was sweating buckets, *literally*. It streaked down his forehead and soaked through his shirt.

"You can't win this one, Carran," Eli spat. "These ghosts are stronger than the ones you snatched from me at JMS."

"I . . . won't . . . give . . . in," Carran said, struggling to get every word out.

The ghosts lurched forward and lifted Carran by her elbows, kicking and screaming. "I tried to warn you," Eli said as they carried her to the forcefield to join the other darkbringers.

We'd put an end to the siege on the school, but it wasn't without injuries on both sides. About half of the godlings had cuts and bruises, and at least a few had broken bones. The same was true of the darkbringers. But my mind was elsewhere. I had to find out why Eleni hadn't come back yet.

Mama, Pam, Dee, Sidda, and the other parents rushed into the main hall. Jayla darted past me, clutching two dolls, headed straight for Eli. "Go ghost mode, Eli, go ghost mode!" she screamed as he scooped her up. Then she was spinning around in the air in invisible arms. I couldn't tell who was giggling harder: her or her dolls.

"Frankie!" Pam said as she and Dee both raced toward her. "We were worried sick about you."

After Sidda checked on Zeran and Billu, she went to talk to the darkbringers. "The Lord of Shadows lied to you," she told them. "The celestials and godlings are not our enemies."

"Are you okay, Maya?" Mama asked, hugging me. When I didn't answer, she pulled away and frowned. "Where's your sister?"

So much had happened in the last few hours, but I forced myself to keep it together. I told Mama that Eleni had gone back to warn Papa and the other celestials that the prisoners from Alsar were on their way. "I have to go find her."

Mama squeezed her eyes shut and shuddered. Then she stared me straight in the eye. "It isn't safe, but . . ." Her voice cracked and broke off.

"I have to go, Mama," I interrupted.

"*But.*" She held up one finger to shush me. "Even though no parent should see their child in danger, I won't stop you from going. You've proven time and time again that you take your guardian responsibilities seriously." Mama sucked in a deep breath. "And your sister needs you."

"I'll bring her back," I said. "I promise."

Mama gave me a sad smile and looked around the hall at the godlings and darkbringers alike moaning in pain. "It seems that I have a lot of work to do here in the meantime."

Frankie, Eli, and Zeran convinced their parents to let them come with me. As we started for the door, Winston, Tay, and Candace blocked our path. "We'll keep everyone safe here," Winston said with a smirk. "We've got this."

"Thanks," I said awkwardly. He'd almost sounded friendly.

"Good luck," he said, then turned on his heels and walked away.

Zeran shrugged, and Frankie shook her head.

"Never thought I would see the day those three started acting like decent godlings," Eli commented.

"Me either," I said as we stepped on the school lawn.

The door that had gotten us to the school reappeared. After some trial and error, we realized that it wouldn't take us to earth, so we decided to return to Azur. Instead of it opening on the old school grounds behind the wrought-iron gate, we exited at the airfield, where months ago we'd ridden horses made of stardust.

I attempted to open a gateway again, and to my dismay, the sparks burned out. "When I try to sense our neighborhood, there's nothing there," I whispered. "It's like a blank space or a hole." I swallowed hard. "I can't sense anything around it. Not Chicago, not Illinois, nothing."

My friends stared at me, but no one said what we all were thinking: What if the celestials had failed, and it was all gone?

"How are we going to get back?" Zeran asked.

Frankie looked at the stables on the edge of the field. "I have an idea."

"Oh no," Eli said, grimacing. "No more horses made out of stardust."

"Perfect," I said as we jogged over to the stables, where the air traffic controller, Gavet, stored vehicles.

"What are you children doing?" came a harsh whisper from the dark. Gavet held up one of the red poles he used to direct air traffic. It was glowing against his scaly skin. "You shouldn't be here. There's a curfew until this mess with the Lord of Shadows and the Alsar prisoners is over."

"Why are you here if there's a curfew?" Zeran asked.

"I don't have a choice, boy," Gavet said, his gaze darting around. "I have to keep the airfield open for those who need assistance to travel between worlds. Not everyone can open a gateway or bend space. Some of us need other means of transportation."

"About those other means . . ." I said. "We need a ride."

Gavet laughed, then he cut himself off as if he'd thought better of it. "You're serious, aren't you?"

"Yes," I said. "We need to get back to earth."

Gavet shrugged. "Who am I to stop a guardian and her friends? The celestials can use all the help they can get, even from kids." He rubbed the tuft of hair on his chin. "I have a flock of peacocks prepped and ready."

"Peacocks," Eli moaned as he slapped his forehead. "Not peacocks."

Frankie frowned. "What's wrong with peacocks?"

"Oh, nothing," Eli squeaked. "Just your run-of-the-mill way to fly."

Soon we were soaring into the sky on the backs of rainbow peacocks, racing against the setting sun. "This is incredible!" Zeran shouted over the wind roaring in our ears.

Eli hugged the neck of his peacock, who protested by squawking the entire flight. "That's not the word I would use to describe it. More like this is *terrifying*."

Maybe if the situation were different, it would have been incredible; instead, my nerves were on edge as we flew closer to earth. I couldn't stop worrying about Papa and Eleni. Papa was not going to be happy that I came back, but I had a good reason. Well, *actually*, I had several: (1) Eleni hadn't met us at the school as planned; (2) someone needed to help deal with the new threat from the Alsar prisoners; and most importantly, (3) the Lord of Shadows had broken through the first perimeter, so the celestials already had their hands full.

It was near sunset when we descended toward our neighborhood. From the sky, everything *almost* looked the same. I could see the mural of the block party on the side of the gyro restaurant, the statue of Jean Baptiste Point du Sable in the park, and the abandoned train tracks next to the supermarket. The third perimeter—the one that Papa had created—formed a shiny dome around the entire neighborhood.

The peacocks set down a few blocks away in an intersection that normally would be busy, but no one was in sight. The whole area was eerily silent. Stray shadows slithered across the sidewalks and crawled up the sides of buildings. I pulled on my peacock's reins to encourage it to move forward, but it only protested and turned in circles.

"You'd think they could have taken us closer," Eli complained.

"I think this is the closest we're going to get," Frankie said, brushing the back of her peacock's head. "They're scared."

When we climbed off the peacocks, they trotted away and took flight.

"Well, well," Black Mamba drawled, stepping in our path. He wore a bright red fedora low on his forehead, but it didn't hide the blood swirling in the whites of his eyes. "Now, why y'all acting all surprised?"

Nice of him to think that we were "acting" surprised.

Surprises were for birthday parties and magic tricks. It was *not* for vampires popping up in your neighborhood, looking thirsty.

"Can't say we're happy to see you," I groaned as my staff began to glow.

"I don't believe that I've properly been introduced to your two friends here." The adze dipped his chin. "I'm called Black Mamba, and this is my enclave."

The other adze transformed in the shadows, where they'd been hidden in their firefly state. They grew into gray masses with specked skin, hunched backs, and sharp talons.

A pack of werehyenas the size of gorillas slinked from behind the buildings nearby. At the same time, shadows flickered across the sky, and a group of darkbringers landed next to the adze. Several dozen elokos pushed past the werehyenas with their jagged teeth bare, then came the prisoners from Alsar—nearly fifty of them. They ranged from small to giant in size, from scaly to *un*scaly. Some had only two arms, whereas others had extra arms and legs. Some had tentacles like Crusher or deadly barbs like Spike. At least half of them had wings. *All of them* had razor-sharp claws.

"I was afraid of this," Zeran mumbled under his breath.

I stood stock-still, unable to speak or move, to even think, as more magical creatures filled the streets—more than I could keep track of. This was much worse than I had expected, but Commander Rovey had warned us that many magical creatures had joined the Lord of Shadows. I just couldn't believe it—or I was in some major denial. Probably both.

Eli gulped. "I don't suppose we can talk this out in a nice, civilized manner?"

Frankie pressed the heels of her hands together, and magic gathered in her palms. "I don't think they're interested in talking much."

Black Mamba grinned. "Y'all already too late anyway. The Lord of Shadows will soon emerge into our world."

I lifted my staff. It felt heavier in my hands than it had my entire time wielding it. Eli called his ghost army. They rose from the ground and through the walls of the surrounding buildings, but we were still outnumbered fifty to one.

Streaks of light cut across the sky, and a person landed in front of us with such force that the ground cracked and dust rose around them. A woman in a purple jumpsuit with lightning striking around her stood with her hands on her hips. Her braids waved in the wind. "Why don't you pick on someone your own size and see what happens?" she said, her voice strong, powerful, commanding.

It wasn't just any woman—*it was her*. I had to pinch myself. It was really her. She was just like from the first issue of the comic books. Oya, the warrior goddess, in the flesh, or um, in the celestial flesh. "Oya." I stuttered. "You—you're really here." Admittedly, I could have come up with something cleverer to say, but I was still in shock. "I mean, you're back."

"It's been a long time—too long," she said as another lightning bolt struck the ground. "I hear the Lord of Shadows is up to his old tricks."

"Unfortunately, he's got some new ones." I gestured to Black Mamba. "And some new friends."

Oya smiled, and I could have melted. She was really here. Like *here, here.* "I have friends too."

Several other celestials landed next to Oya. Orunmila, the orisha of wisdom with a golden disc around his head. Okó, the hunter, who I'd read about in Oya's comic books. Mama Wata, who had the biggest python I had ever seen wrapped around her neck. Then there were the other celestials. The big man, John Henry. Harriett Tubman, the celestial best known for helping to free people on the Underground Railroad. And many more celestials that I didn't recognize.

"Enough chitchat and socializing," Black Mamba said as he transformed into his natural state. "We've been waiting for our day to destroy the celestials for a long time."

"Go." Oya opened her arms wide, and her feet lifted from the ground. "We'll take it from here."

Under any other circumstance, it would've been a dream

to fight side by side with the great Oya, but I had to find Eleni.

The adze were the first to rush at us, with the were-hyenas close on their heels. Oya and the other orishas were a blur of bright light as they fought back the army. It was pure chaos.

"You don't have to tell me twice," Eli said as his ghosts closed ranks around us.

We fought off attackers the entire two blocks before running into Papa's veil. I pressed my hand against it, feeling the familiar hum, then I stepped back and slashed it with my staff. I'd torn a hole in the only thing keeping the Lord of Shadows at bay.

TWENTY-SEVEN

TRAPPED IN A MAZE

I STARED AT THE tear, almost in shock that it'd been that easy, but then again, Eleni and I were the only people with the magic to destroy Papa's veils. That was why the Lord of Shadows needed us to bring down the one between the human and the Dark worlds.

Eli's ghosts filed through the tear first, and we followed close behind. Once we were inside, I realized what we'd seen from the sky was only an illusion. We had stepped into a nightmare. Our neighborhood, the place where I'd spent my entire life, was little more than a shell. Even in the fading evening light, everything was gray—the streets, the buildings, the stop signs, the trees, the snow, the parked cars. The air smelled wet and moldy, like something slowly rotting. Black lightning etched across the sky.

"This is . . . *not good*," Frankie remarked.

"At least the veil around the neighborhood is still up," Zeran said optimistically.

Papa said it was only a matter of time before the Lord of Shadows freed himself, and time was almost up. I knew one thing for sure. This would be the last battle between the other celestials and the Lord of Shadows. Their millennia-old war would finally come to an end. I swiped the staff across the tear in the veil. Blue sparks poured from my hand, and the tear stitched itself back together.

"Go scope out the neighborhood," Eli told his ghosts.

"Roger that," one of the ghosts said.

"Aye, Captain." Another ghost saluted before they scattered in every direction and disappeared.

"They could be off haunting a house or a graveyard, but they're here representing," Eli said proudly.

"They are pretty awesome to be made of . . . What's the paranormal word for it—*ectoplasm*," Frankie said.

"I'm impressed." Eli slapped her on the shoulder. "There's hope for you yet."

I turned away from the veil. Time to get down to business. "We have to find Eleni."

Zeran peered around the gloomy night. "She could be anywhere."

A dozen thoughts raced through my head. Why hadn't Eleni come back? She could've cut through the veil the same as me. Did she have a chance to warn Papa and the other celestials before the prisoners from Alsar arrived? Where was she now?

I concentrated on my sister, but all I could feel was the coldness of the winter night and something much worse. Beneath the cold, there was nothing but despair. It was like everything in the world was wrong, backward, upside down. That was what the Lord of Shadows wanted me to feel, but I resisted. I wasn't about to lose hope. "Let's start at JMS," I said. "Papa and the other celestials would be there to hold the second perimeter, so she's likely with them."

We dipped in and out of the shadows, dodging packs of werehyenas patrolling the street. They were positively giddy, with their noses to the ground as they sniffed everything and everywhere. There was the whooshing sound of wingbeats overhead, and we ducked out of sight of darkbringer scouts.

"Time to go ghost mode," Eli said, reaching for Frankie.

Frankie smiled as she took his hand. Sensing what was coming next, my staff turned back into a ring, and I slipped it on my finger. Frankie grabbed my hand, then I reached for Zeran, who tilted his head to the side. "Um, what are you doing?" he asked.

"Trust us," I said, winking at him.

He smiled and took my hand. "You don't even have to ask. You know I trust you."

I felt bad about doubting him earlier. Zeran was my

friend, but if I was being honest, he sometimes made my heart skip a beat when I looked at him too long. There, I admitted it. I liked him. I wasn't sure how much I liked him, but I was annoyed that Gail Galanis and half the students at JMS also liked him. I wasn't ready to face what that meant.

Eli pulled us into ghost mode. We could see ourselves, but we also could see through each other. "Whoa," Zeran said, staring at his hand. "This is *different*."

Cheers rang out in the night, then flames burned across the sky. The third perimeter was on fire, but it was still holding—*barely*.

We almost ran smack into three darkbringers walking tazars that made Ogun's bloodhound, General, look like a poodle. Instead of fur, they were covered in green scales with sharp spikes across their backs. One of the beasts jerked his head toward us and growled. We stopped, holding our breath. None of us were in a position to fight, but we would if we had to. A second later, a rat scurried between Frankie's feet and disappeared into the shadows. The tazar pulled against its leash, his gaze following the rodent's path. We were no better than it: rats trapped in a maze.

"Look everywhere," one of the darkbringers barked. "Find the little aziza before she causes trouble."

"Eleni," I said. They were looking for her, which meant she had to be okay for now.

I heard a voice that stopped me in my tracks. I couldn't move, couldn't talk, couldn't breathe. Chills shot down my spine. "I am almost free, *friends*," said the Lord of Shadows. His words vibrated inside my head. "This is a joyous occasion, one that will be marked by the death of my brethren."

"Maya, what's wrong?" Frankie whispered, snapping me out of the daze.

My heart thundered against my chest. The Lord of Shadows was almost free, and he was planning to kill the other celestials. He was planning to kill Papa. But for some strange reason, I couldn't bring myself to tell my friends. I bit my tongue, confused. "Nothing—let's keep going."

By the time we reached JMS, I was convinced that I had imagined the voice. That was the only thing that made sense. I was tired, hungry, and more than a little scared. When I saw the perimeter still intact around our school, I let out a shaky breath. It was a swirling mist that had sporadic spots of brilliant light that weaved together into countless lines to form a net. The whole thing was pulsing like a heartbeat.

Eli stared up at the light over the main building. *"Nana?"*

I swallowed the lump in my throat and nodded. I could feel the celestials' magic. It radiated in the air, brushing against our skin. And I knew which one was Papa—I could sense him. He was floating over the gym.

I bit down a scream as purple and black ribbons pierced through the mist and struck Papa and the other celestials— Yemoja, Nana Buruku, Oshun, Ogun, Eshu, Shangó, Obatala, Principal Ollie, and a dozen more. Sparks of magic flew everywhere as they fought back, but it was no use. The ribbons lashed out again and again, and the celestials' light grew dimmer. The Lord of Shadows was draining the life from them.

Frankie inhaled a sharp breath. "We're too late."

"We have to go," Zeran said, yanking on my hand.

"No," I whispered in shock. This couldn't be happening.

When the Lord of Shadows fully emerged from the mist, he was as I remembered: tall with an angular face, skin the color of the moon, glowing violet eyes. His arms were long and crooked like tree branches, and his upper body was abnormally slender. The rest of him was made of hundreds of writhing ribbons. As the second perimeter disintegrated, some of his ribbons reached out and struck the veil around our neighborhood. It lit up for one fleeting moment before blinking out.

The magical creatures came at once, flooding the streets and sky alike. Darkbringers, adze, elokos, werehyenas, werewolves, elves, centaurs, bogeymen. The prisoners from Alsar. Oya and the other celestials had failed to stop them. Nulan swooped down from the sky and kneeled before the Lord of Shadows, and I had an urge to whack her with my staff. The rest of his army kneeled too, their heads bowed.

"This world is yours for the taking, my lord," Nulan groveled.

"Of course it is," the Lord of Shadows cooed, his voice ancient.

Some of the magical creatures laughed nervously, glancing around at each other. The Lord of Shadows turned to the darkbringer kneeling next to Nulan. "See that the other celestials and their supporters do not disturb me. I will take care of them in due time."

"Of course, my lord," the darkbringer said, getting to his feet. He barked some orders, and half of the Lord of Shadows' forces left with him. They must have been talking about Oya, Orunmila, Mama Wata, and the others.

"Where's the girl?" the Lord of Shadows hissed.

"She's hiding in her house," Nulan said, amused. "Putting up quite a fight, so I've been told. Shall I have her brought to you?"

"No." The Lord of Shadows smiled. "I shall stretch my legs and go for a little stroll."

"What legs?" Eli whispered.

This was *not* the time to be cracking jokes.

"As you wish, my lord," Nulan said, her head still bent.

The Lord of Shadows glared down his nose. "Well, take me to her, Tyana! She's *your* niece."

Nulan sprang to her feet. "Of course, my lord."

"*Un-freaking-believable*," Frankie groaned. "She's the absolute worst!"

How could Nulan be so willing to give Eleni up without a second thought? A memory edged into the back of my mind. In it, Tyana Nulan stood over me with a look of triumph. She'd said something I couldn't remember. *Why can't I remember it?*

With Nulan leading the way, the magical creatures surrounded the Lord of Shadows. He glided forward with the celestials trapped in his ribbons. "Behold your mighty gods," the Lord of Shadows spat. "Not so mighty now."

I gritted my teeth, wanting nothing more than to take the fight to him, but I couldn't bring myself to move a muscle. "We have to do something," I said, swallowing down my tears.

"What can we do?" Frankie mumbled. "Even the celestials couldn't stop him."

Zeran frowned. "Why does he want Eleni?"

"Isn't it obvious?" I snapped, frustrated. "She has the power to open gateways across the universe. He would have the ability to travel anywhere instantly. Soon the whole universe will be under his control. I have to stop him."

Eli coughed. "You mean, we have to stop him."

"We're your ride or die," Zeran reminded me.

"Though I prefer not dying today," added Frankie.

I squeezed my friends' hands and pushed down my

nerves. We had to *do* something, but Frankie was right. What real chance did we have if the celestials had already failed? They weren't dead yet, but they were dying.

Still invisible, we followed at a distance as the Lord of Shadows paraded around our neighborhood with the celestials in his ribbons. That was why he wanted to stretch his *nonexistent* legs. He wanted to gloat.

When we arrived on my block, the magical creatures had gathered on the street in front of my house. They perched in trees and on fences and rooftops—hundreds of them. The moon shined so brightly that it looked like daytime. Shadows wound together to form something akin to a stage in the center of the crowd, and the Lord of Shadows' black and purple ribbons propelled him on top of it.

I itched to fight. I needed to do something, anything, but I forced myself to stay put. Captain Nulan and a handful of darkbringers climbed onto the stage and stood on either side of the Lord of Shadows. I wouldn't get two steps before one of them or someone from the crowd stopped me.

Eli was ghastly pale again as his ghosts gathered around the edges of the crowd and peered from behind the curtains in the houses.

"Bring the girl," the Lord of Shadows commanded, and my heart dropped.

Everything had gone wrong.

A darkbringer with wings the color of blood dragged Eleni, kicking and screaming, to the stage. "Let go of me!" she yelled as fairy dust started to shimmer against her skin, but the darkbringer quickly snapped a collar around her neck. I'd seen collars like that before. They prevented someone from using their magic.

"Do not be afraid, child," the Lord of Shadows said as one of his ribbons inched toward her. "I will give you one chance to save yourself from an unfortunate fate."

Eleni kept struggling, but she didn't speak. Instead, she glanced up at her auntie—at Captain Nulan—as if begging her to help.

"Some of the celestials have run away like the cowards I already knew them to be," the Lord of Shadows said. "They've taken a great deal of the humans with them. You're going to help me find every single world where a celestial might be hiding."

Eleni laughed, and it was one sharp note. Captain Nulan curled her lip in disgust, but Eleni straightened her back, her wings shimmering in the moonlight. She tilted her chin up defiantly. "I would rather die ten times over than help you."

The Lord of Shadows smiled, and somehow his gaunt face looked even narrower. "You forget that I have the amplifier that can steal your guardian powers, but then again, I don't need it." He turned toward the crowd and raised his voice. "Why would I need the amplifier when I have a guardian who already serves me?"

I frowned, not understanding. Who was the Lord of Shadows talking about? There were only three guardians: Papa, Eleni, and me. And there was no way either of us would help him under any circumstance.

"That guardian is here now," he continued. "Among my subjects."

The darkbringers and other magical creatures glanced around, searching for this mysterious guardian. I looked, too, but my friends were staring at me.

I could feel the hum of magic underneath my skin. It was whispering something to me. I let go of Frankie's hand, and Zeran and I became visible again. The crowd was so thick that no one noticed us.

"Maya, what are you doing?" Frankie hissed next to my ear.

My lips moved, but I couldn't answer her. A familiar, slippery voice like birdsong played in my mind—Nulan's voice. I thought about the last time I had seen her, right before she escaped, leaving Frankie and me on the barren planet. There was a slice of time missing in my memory. One minute I had been fighting Nulan, and the next, she was gone. Why would she leave without finishing me off?

"Frankie, was Maya ever alone with Captain Nulan?" Zeran asked quickly.

"Um, I . . . I don't know," Frankie stuttered. "What's wrong with her?"

Eli's disembodied voice was grave as he said, "It's fairy magic."

I shook my head, but even as I did, my whole body tingled. "No," I whispered.

Zeran tried desperately to pull me through the crowd, away from the stage.

"Maya Janine Abeola, come join your sister," the Lord of Shadows called.

I stopped in my tracks and met Zeran's eyes. He was shaking his head, his black eyes filled with tears. I snatched my hand out of his grasp, my chest heaving up and down. I had to go to the Lord of Shadows. I wanted nothing more than to do as he commanded. But that wasn't right. What was I thinking? What was I doing?

Zeran backed away and disappeared into the crowd. I turned around, and people parted to make a path for me. Papa moaned like someone had stolen his whole world, but still, he couldn't free himself. "Baby girl, no!" he screamed before the Lord of Shadows' ribbons completely wrapped him in a cocoon, cutting off his plea.

I removed the ring from my finger, and it turned into

a staff again. The god symbols flashed once before going completely dark. As I drew closer to the Lord of Shadows, the staff began to crumble beneath my fingers until nothing was left.

TWENTY-EIGHT

ENDGAME

MY LEGS WERE heavy as I climbed the steps to the stage and stood face-to-face with the Lord of Shadows. Every muscle in my body screamed, *Wrong, wrong, wrong*, but I only lowered my eyes and stared at my feet. How could it be wrong when I was destined to serve the Lord of Shadows? Why had I ever resisted? "Your wish is my command, my lord," I said. *Wrong, wrong, wrong.*

The Lord of Shadows laughed, and it was a cackle that grated against my ears. His ribbons hissed and snapped as they slithered across the stage. "Of course, child, of course."

"What have you done to my sister?" Eleni yelled.

I registered her voice, but it was like listening to her while wearing earplugs.

"She's finally come to her senses," Captain Nulan said. "Haven't you, *Maya*?"

I nodded slowly, though I had no idea what she meant. I only knew that I was supposed to agree, and that felt wrong. My head was throbbing, and my eyes tingled.

"You did this," Eleni snapped. "You used fairy magic to force her to serve the Lord of Shadows."

Captain Nulan's eyes narrowed into daggers. "You mean I helped her see reason. You would be wise to follow her lead before it's too late."

"Maya, please, fight Auntie Tyana's magic!" Eleni screamed with tears in her eyes. "You're stronger than her."

My thoughts slowly spun in a circle as I remembered Eleni standing in the hallway at the community center and Miss Nichelle's glazed-over eyes and slack jaw. She had accidentally lost control of her fairy magic. *Fairy magic.* Nulan had used fairy magic on me.

The Lord of Shadows' ribbons lowered him so his face was level with Nulan's. His violet-colored eyes glowed more intensely. "Silence your niece, or I will."

"Yes, my lord . . ." Nulan stuttered before stalking across the stage and grabbing Eleni's arm. "Another word, and it'll be your last."

The Lord of Shadows turned to the crowd and let out a hoarse laugh that sounded like someone crumpling up old wallpaper. "Friends, no longer will you be relegated to the swamps and forests and shadows." He gestured to a pack of werehyenas standing on their hind legs. "You can roam free without having to curb your appetites."

The crowd of magical creatures cheered, and the were-hyenas yelped and cackled in excitement. I frowned. My head throbbed even more. I knew that I had to fight Nulan's fairy magic, but it was hard to think straight.

The Lord of Shadows looked up at the sky where some of his ribbons still had the celestials entangled—where he had Papa. "The time has finally come for me to make good on my promise and rid the universe of the celestials."

The light faded from one of the celestials, then another and another. Who was gone? I couldn't tell from here. They were too high up. Tears pricked my eyes. What if one was Papa? The ribbons that had drunk the celestials' lives mul-tiplied, and the Lord of Shadows' violet eyes grew brighter.

"No!" Eleni screamed.

Nulan grabbed the metal collar around Eleni's neck and yanked her closer. "Shut up!"

"Stop it!" Eleni screamed again, and this time the Lord of Shadows turned his attention to her.

My heart dropped as his ribbons slithered toward Eleni, hissing and snapping.

He was going to drain the life out of her like he was doing to Papa and the other celestials. I couldn't let that happen. I had to stop him. My fingers twitched as I struggled against

Nulan's magic. It pulsed in my ears, trying desperately to lure me back into a trance. Gritting my teeth, I pushed hard. It was a tug-of-war, but the rope was my mind. I screamed inside my head, and suddenly something snapped. My legs almost buckled, but I forced myself to stay standing.

"I am reconsidering your usefulness, Eleni," the Lord of Shadows said as several of his ribbons reared back, like cobras ready to strike my sister. She squeezed her eyes shut.

"No!" I lurched forward on wobbly legs. The Lord of Shadows glared at me, but I didn't back down. I had only one shot, and I had to make it count. "Why have one guardian when you can have two, *my lord*? My sister will come around eventually."

Eleni opened her eyes. She looked miserable as she swiped tears from her cheeks, which only made my betrayal that more convincing. If it wasn't for her, I might still be under Nulan's control. "Maya, please," she begged, her voice barely above a whisper. "Fight it."

I made sure to keep my face clear of emotions. I had to pretend that I didn't care. "Stop making this harder than it needs to be."

"It's just as I promised, my lord," Nulan said, eagerly. "My control over the girl is absolute."

"We shall see, Tyana." The Lord of Shadows flourished his long, spiny hand at one of his generals. "Give the guardian your prod. Let her prove her loyalty or die where she stands." He turned to me with his glowing eyes. "Punish Eleni for her disobedience."

I swallowed my fear as the general—a darkbringer with a bull face and flared nostrils—removed the blue metal prod from a clip at his waist and offered it to me. I snatched it out of his hand like I was ready to get this over with. "You're always messing up, Eleni," I said, stalking over to where she was still next to Nulan. "Just like when we opened gateways at that garbage dump and yours utterly failed."

I held my breath, desperately hoping she remembered the time our gateways had intersected. For a brief moment, there had been a bubble of spinning god symbols. If we couldn't trap the Lord of Shadows outside of the universe, maybe we could trap him in a slice of space *inside* it. Maybe it would work, or maybe it wouldn't, but we had to try something.

Eleni frowned at me, and I could tell she was trying to work it out. I pressed the prod to the metal collar around her neck and looked into her eyes. *Remember, Eleni, please.* "It seems we're at a crossroads, Sister, an intersection," I spat. *Please remember.* "Your time is up."

As I reared the prod back, a buzz of electricity vibrated up my arm. Someone slammed into me. I hit the stage hard, and the crowd erupted into chaos. The Lord of Shadows was on the move, his writhing ribbons spinning and twisting.

Eleni was being pulled off the stage, dragged backward by invisible hands. Eli! But before they could escape, Nulan sprang to action. She lifted her hand and blew fairy dust. Eli was in ghost mode, but the fairy dust highlighted his outline next to Eleni. One of the darkbringer generals tackled Eli, and they fell off the stage into the crowd. *No, no, no.* This wasn't going at all how I had planned.

As I climbed to my feet, a ball of magic hit Nulan squarely in the chest. She grunted once before she fell to her knees. I looked back in time to see Frankie climbing down from a tree. Then Zeran's animation roared as it pounded through the crowd.

The Lord of Shadows was at the center of the stage now, and his generals had moved around the edges to protect him. In the gaps between them, I saw Oya, Orunmila, Miss Lucille, and Miss Ida leading another group of magical creatures, facing off against the Lord of Shadows' army. The Bigfoot clan, standing tall with their axes. The aziza—Eleni's people—with their shimmering skin and luminescent wings. Eli's ghosts. Unicorns, phoenixes. Elokos—possibly the vegetarian ones from Azur—riding on the backs of dragons. And Zeran's dad—Commander Rovey—with a group of darkbringer Resistance fighters. They had finally broken through the Lord of Shadows' forces.

Eleni pulled the collar from around her neck. I had

unlocked it before Eli slammed into me and ruined my plan. "Thanks, Sis!"

"Kill them all!" the Lord of Shadows roared. "Leave no one alive or answer to me."

With his attention on Oya, Miss Lucille, Miss Ida, and the others, I poured my magic into the prod and transformed it into a sword, then I bent space. I knew it was risky to try again, but I needed to move faster than the Lord of Shadows. A split second later, I was hurtling through the air, swinging the sword. But before I could do any damage, one of the Lord of Shadows' ribbons grabbed me from behind.

"Did you really think that you, a mere child, could stand in my way?" the Lord of Shadows bellowed. "You'll die with the rest of your family."

A sharp pain shot through my ribs as his ribbons squeezed the air out of my lungs. I heard Eleni screaming my name and felt a brush of her fairy magic. It was just enough to distract the Lord of Shadows. I swung the sword. It soared through the air and cut several of his ribbons.

The Lord of Shadows cried out as light spread across his shadows. He lost his grasp on the celestials, and their limp, almost lifeless bodies fell to the ground. I was already bending space again. This time I landed in front of the Lord of Shadows while Eleni was still behind him.

"You're going to regret that, guardian," he growled.

"I don't think so," I said as a gateway formed between us. "Now, Eleni!"

My sister stood on the opposite end of the stage with her arms wide as she opened a gateway of her own. A gateway was two-dimensional in the physical world, but in the nonphysical world—basically, the space where dark energy flowed—it was a tunnel between two locations. I directed my gateway to intersect with Eleni's, where the Lord of Shadows stood.

A burst of god symbols spun around him—first only a few, then hundreds of them. He thrashed his ribbons out, batting them away, but they weaved around faster, dodging his attack. "What is this nonsense?"

"This nonsense is the end of you," I said as sweat beaded on my forehead.

I could feel him resisting, pushing back against the god symbols. Blood trickled from my nose at the strain of holding the gateway open. Eleni wasn't faring much better. Her face was twisted in pain. The god symbols started to link together in chains around the Lord of Shadows.

He yelled so loud that his voice cracked the stage in two. Eleni fell to her knees, but she didn't lose her gateway. "I was the universe's first creation, long before the celestials, and I will endure long after they are gone."

He was expanding now, growing bigger and taller. His

purple and black ribbons lashed out and broke some of the chains of god symbols. Pain cut across my temples, and I gritted my teeth. It wasn't working—the bubble of god symbols was only half-complete.

"My gateway's starting to collapse," Eleni shouted.

"We were always going to arrive at this point, Maya," the Lord of Shadows said, his voice laced with amusement. "You lose, and I win."

My knees trembled, but I forced myself to hold on a bit longer. This was it. This was my endgame. "If we fail, there will always be people who stand up for what's right no matter how much you try to intimidate us."

"You have your father's stubbornness," the Lord of Shadows said. "Too bad you are irredeemable. I could have taught you how to use that darkness inside you, child."

The thought of ever serving the Lord of Shadows sent a chill down my spine. I'd have rather stayed in after-school math tutoring with Ms. Vanderbilt for the rest of my life or eaten the horrible lumpy vanilla pudding in the cafeteria or listened to some of Winston's bad rap on YouTube. No way, absolutely no way, would I ever turn into one of his cronies.

There was a flash of white light on the stage, and suddenly Papa was there in his human form. My heart swelled with joy. Papa was alive. He was okay! He stood tall with the wind blowing through his locs, his skin glowing with celestial light. "Fortunately, she has better role models,"

Papa said, then he opened a gateway that intersected with Eleni's and mine.

More god symbols materialized—thousands of them. They exploded in the air and spun around the Lord of Shadows at a dizzying pace. I focused all my energy on the gateway. It was our last chance to stop him. With Papa's magic added to our own, the god symbols built the links faster than the Lord of Shadows could destroy them.

Eleni got to her feet. "This is for Mama, Genu, and Kimala."

"And for all the other people you hurt!" I added.

The Lord of Shadows yelled one last time before the god symbols completely engulfed him in a bubble of pure light and cut off his scream. The bubble shrank and disappeared inside the space where our three gateways intersected.

I swept away the sweat on my forehead. I couldn't believe it—we'd done it. He was gone. Guardians of the veil: one. Lord of Shadows: a giant zero.

"He's dead!" someone yelled. "The Lord of Shadows is dead."

Eli and Frankie fist pumped and cheered while Zeran waved at me from his perch on top of a roof. The fighting around us slowed as people on both sides stopped to stare at Papa, Eleni, and me. I didn't have the heart to tell them that the Lord of Shadows wasn't dead, but he wouldn't be coming back either. Some of the magical creatures who'd chosen to fight for him retreated. I couldn't believe that the celestials were just letting them go. There had to be more to it.

"What a clever idea to trap the Lord of Shadows using intersecting gateways," Papa mused as he pulled us in for a hug.

"Maya thought of it," Eleni volunteered.

"I couldn't have done it without you and Papa," I said, squeezing her hand.

It was over, really over. I leaned against Papa, my shoulders sagging with relief. The celestials—Principal Ollie, Ogun, Yemoja, Nana, Oya, and the others—fought against the last of the Lord of Shadows' forces. They were winning, but my heart dropped when I didn't see Shangó, aka Mr. Jenkins, our science teacher. I got the idea about the intersecting gateways from his dark energy theory. Was he one of the celestials who the Lord of Shadows had absorbed?

I glanced around our neighborhood. Everything was still ash gray, but the wayward shadows were retreating. Although I was relieved, I realized that nothing would ever be the same—not after today. I couldn't just go back to the life I had before I found out about the celestials and the magical world. And maybe the Lord of Shadows was gone, but there were magical creatures who believed in what he stood for.

The veil between worlds was still on the verge of falling, but I would worry about that another day. "Let's go get Mama."

TWENTY-NINE

THE VEIL

ELENI AND I stepped onto the front porch as a fresh batch of snow sprinkled our neighborhood. Now that we'd defeated the Lord of Shadows, all the things that had turned gray were back to normal. The sky, the trees, the stop sign. Latesha's red curtains, Mr. Mason's blue shutters, the Lees' mural, the Patels' elephant statue, the Okekes' bright yellow birdhouse. Well, the greystones were still gray, but they were supposed to be.

Little kids ran up and down the sidewalk, laughing. A snowball smacked against the wall next to my head. "Sorry!" Billu said as he crouched beside a tree. He grinned sheepishly before rejoining the snowball fight.

His mom, Sidda, along with dozens of other darkbringers, had wanted to stay in the human world, which had caused much debate among the celestials, godlings, and our human families.

"It's nice to see new faces in the neighborhood," Mama said as she and Papa stepped out of the house behind us. "Glad to see some familiar faces, too." She waved at Latesha, who was working on her latest masterpiece: a snowman wearing armor made out of aluminum foil.

"This is how it should be," Papa replied. "Darkbringers and humans sharing the same world."

"Do you think the orisha council will rule in favor of destroying the veil?" I asked Papa. I had mixed feelings—not about the veil coming down, but that without it, I wouldn't be a guardian anymore. I liked helping Papa, but if destroying the veil could unite our fractured world, it was a small price to pay. Besides, I liked the idea of spending my spare time opening gateways to faraway places. Though I wouldn't mind traveling the old-fashioned way sometimes.

"It isn't up to our council alone," Papa explained. "The meeting today will be with all the councils across the human world and representatives from the Dark." Papa paused, glancing at the sky. "But I suspect the veil will come down one way or another."

"It's long overdue if you ask me," Mama said.

Eleni pulled the hood of her coat up and stuffed her hands in her pockets. "I can't wait until spring's here. It'll be a fresh beginning for everyone."

"Where should we go for spring break?" Mama asked as Papa wrapped an arm around her shoulders. "Normally, I would recommend something on the beach, but we should broaden our horizons. There's the whole universe to explore, after all."

"How about the asteroid belt between Jupiter and Mars?" Papa asked, excited. "The merchants there have some of the most exquisite and rare trinkets from across the universe, and the food is intergalactic class. There's this chef who makes the best barbecue seaweed popsicles." Mama and Eleni wrinkled their noses, but Papa only laughed. "What? Don't knock it before you try it. It's the perfect amount of sweetness and spiciness."

"We'll take your word for it," Mama said, grimacing.

"I've heard that there's a cloud off the coast of Azur that has a wonderful day spa," Eleni suggested. "We should go there for facials and massages."

Mama squealed. "Now that's a vacation I would love."

"How about you two go to the spa, and we'll check out that asteroid?" I said.

Papa looked at our neighborhood and let out a deep sigh. "I haven't known the world without the veil for a very long time. It's going to take some getting used to."

"One step at a time," Mama said, squeezing his hand.

Across the street, Latesha was draping tinsel on her snowman. One of the darkbringer kids levitated nearby and handed her alternating colors. "I knew there was something special about this neighborhood," she mused as her cousin LJ played on his phone.

"You always said it, cuz," he replied absently. "You were right."

Not everyone had come back to the neighborhood, but the humans that had were magically sworn to secrecy, which meant they couldn't reveal the truth even if they tried. The few neighbors who didn't like the idea of living among magical creatures decided to move. Predictably, the celestials had erased their memories along with the rest of the humans' outside of the sanctuaries. They'd forgotten about magic, the threat from the Lord of Shadows, and that they'd been temporarily relocated to another planet.

I thought that was extreme, but the celestials insisted that it was for the best. There were still people like Gail Galanis who couldn't be affected by magic, but more than likely, no one would believe them if they went raving about werehyenas and a man made of shadows.

"Yemoja and some of the other celestials will be leaving soon," Papa said.

"What about Oya?" I tugged at the red-and-gold sash around my waist. I still hadn't worked up the courage to talk to her yet. "Is she leaving too?"

Papa smiled broadly. "She's going to stick around a

little longer. She's remodeling the old house on Forty-Ninth Street. The one everyone says is haunted."

Eleni and I looked at each other. That was the house we'd seen on the crossroads that had held the Lord of Shadows back. It didn't bring up good memories. Maybe Oya being there would change its reputation.

While Papa and Mama continued to the community center, Eleni and I went to Eli's place, where he, Frankie, and Zeran had been playing video games all morning. Auntie Bae was bustling around the kitchen with Jayla on her heels. "Why can't I take my dolls to school with me?"

"Because they never stop talking," Auntie Bae said.

"Oh, come on, Auntie Bae," one of the dolls Jayla was clutching cooed. "We'll make excellent company at school. We can be teachers' assistants."

"I'm somewhat of a history buff," the second doll said. "I've been watching TV every night for a month."

"We've heard," Auntie Bae mumbled.

Upstairs, Eli, Frankie, and Zeran were huddled on the floor in front of a video game. The three of them had teamed up to go on a quest to save a powerful mage kidnapped by an evil overlord bent on world domination. "We don't have anything like this back home," Zeran said as his fingers flew across the buttons of the controller.

"You don't have to be so good at it," Eli groaned.

"We would've been past this level already if you two would've used the indestructible suits I made," Frankie said, pausing the game. "There was a sixty-one percent chance that they wouldn't have melted our bones."

"And a thirty-nine percent chance they would have," Eli shot back. "I don't know about you, but I like my bones unmelted. Thank you very much."

"It is time already?" Zeran asked, blinking up at me. He looked nervous.

I wanted to reassure him, but I had no clue how the celestials would rule. They were so strict about everything—and they thought they always knew what was best. "Whatever happens, the five of us have to make a pact right here." I looked at each of them, taking in their faces. "We'll always be there for each other, no matter what. Deal?"

"Deal," everyone said as we executed a five-way fist bump.

Frankie thrust her phone into my hand, and I read the headline from the *Azurian Times-Journal*: **NOTORIOUS EX-PEACEKEEPER "BUTCHER" CONTINUES TO EVADE AUTHORITIES**. "She's still out there," Frankie said.

I cracked my knuckles. "We'll find her. She can't hide forever."

"My ghosts are on the lookout too," Eli added. "They have a whisper network across the universe. It's only a matter of time before one of them spots her."

Frankie adjusted her glasses and wiped her eyes. "Let's hope so."

"The council meeting should be starting any moment now," Eleni said, opening a gateway.

As we stepped through Eleni's gateway, which looked like a spring day in a magical forest, I couldn't get over how this was my life now. I had a sister—A SISTER—and she was pretty awesome. Mama and Papa were okay. My friends were okay. We'd defeated the Lord of Shadows and his cronies.

The hallway outside of the gods' realm was crowded with people. The cranky Johnston twins were directing traffic. We rubbed shoulders with elokos, aziza, darkbringers, adze, werehyenas, the Bigfoot clan, and many more magical creatures. Our human families had come too.

"This is going to be interesting," Eli said as a werewolf growled at a werehyena.

"Very," Frankie mused, watching a group of adze in firefly form swarm by us.

Once we were inside, we saw countless bleachers that stretched to the stars. I spotted Mama chatting with Frankie's moms, Dee and Pam. Next to them, Zeran's mom, Sidda, was talking to Principal Ollie. His father, Commander Rovey, had returned to the Dark world. Zeran acted like he didn't care, but it didn't take a rocket scientist to figure out that he was still mad at his father. Maybe it would take some time for them to work it out, or maybe they never would. No matter what, I would be here for Zeran if he ever wanted to talk about it.

The orisha council sat on their thrones as we found seats. Eli's grandmother, Nana Buruku, who embodied the spirit of the earth, sat on a throne covered in lush green vines. She wore a billowing purple dress, and her gray hair was done up in braids. Next to her sat Oshun, the orisha of beauty, looking, well, *beautiful*. She wore rings around her neck of alternating silver and gold, and her throne was bedecked in jewels.

Sitting in the middle was Eshu, the god of balance. His throne was swirling light and dark in perfect harmony. Ogun was next with his hound, General, lying across his feet. His throne was all metal. Finally, my eyes landed on the last throne, and my chest tightened. Papa sat there, newly elected to the council. His throne wasn't a throne at all. It was an exact copy of the old blue recliner at home. I smiled, remembering all the times I sat on his lap in that chair, listening to his wild stories. It turned out that they weren't so wild after all.

Yemoja swept forward with waves lapping at her ankles and bowed to the council members. "I hereby relinquish my claim over this sanctuary and leave it in your capable hands."

"Thank you, Yemoja," Nana said before turning to the

crowd. "Across the world, each council is holding a similar meeting with the people of their sanctuary. It is our hope that today we will start the process of healing old wounds and forming lasting friendships."

"To that end, we have decided that there must be changes if we are to move forward in peace now that the Lord of Shadows is gone," Oshun continued. "We know that the magical creatures have grown tired of living in the shadows, but you've seen firsthand what chaos your presence brings to the human world. We don't have all the answers, but we believe the best course of action will be to invite representatives from each of your species to meet with us to find a solution that will satisfy everyone."

There was some rumbling in the crowd, but no one spoke up. It was a big step forward that the celestials were willing to listen to the same creatures that the Lord of Shadows had recruited to his side.

"As for the veil, we can all agree that it must come down eventually," Eshu said. "But the human world is not ready to know of magic. It might take a few more centuries before it fails on its own, now that the Lord of Shadows isn't wounding it. For the time being, we will leave it intact."

Some of the darkbringers in the crowd shouted their protests, but Papa spoke up next. "Even with the veil still standing, we will permanently leave gateways open between the human world and the Dark, so each of you can come and go as you please. Darkbringers will be welcome to stay in any of our sanctuaries or on Azur if they so choose."

I glanced at Zeran, who was beaming. He winked at me, and I ducked my head. This was much better news than I could have hoped for. Zeran would be permanently staying in our neighborhood. Eventually, I would have to deal with this whole liking him thing, but not today or tomorrow, or even next week. Nope. Not happening. I could face off against the Lord of Shadows, but by far, figuring out that you liked one of your friends was way harder.

After the assembly, people slowly started to leave the gods' realm, but some of us hung back. Charlie, the kishi peacekeeper, apologized to Frankie for not answering her calls.

"Have you ever heard of black bean burgers?" Eli was asking a group of elokos. "Hands down better than human flesh, I promise."

Eleni chatted excitedly with her friends about the upcoming school dance.

Zeran sat on the bleachers with Billu, the two catching up.

"Hey, nice sash," someone said, and I inhaled a sharp breath. "Your father tracked me down halfway across the universe and told me that you were my biggest fan."

Oya was wearing a purple-and-silver jumpsuit, and her

braids were pulled back into a ponytail. I tried to say something, anything.

"I'm your biggest fan!" I blurted out before I realized we'd already covered that part. Nice one, Abeola.

Oya grinned. "I must admit, it's strange to come back after all this time and learn that my children have written comic books about my adventures."

"But they're amazing adventures," I said a little too excitedly.

"You've had some amazing adventures of your own," she mused.

I smiled at that and glanced at my shoes. "I guess so."

"Come by to see me sometime," Oya said. "I have a few stories that didn't make it into the comic books."

I swallowed down a squeal. "I'd like that."

When Oya left, I had to take several deep breaths to get my head straight. Mama wrapped an arm around my shoulders as she, Papa, and Eleni joined me. We'd gone through a lot together, and I had the feeling that we would have many more adventures. I might not have been a guardian anymore, but the world would always need heroes.

ACKNOWLEDGMENTS

I am truly grateful for the many years I spent living and dreaming in the fantastical world of *Maya and the Rising Dark*. When I set out to write this series, I wanted to make it a little dark and a little scary, but I also wanted to make sure the pages were full of hope, moments of joy, family, and friendship. The characters have made me laugh out loud, cry, and cheer, and have kept me up late into the night.

Maya has the support of her family, friends, and community throughout her adventure, and I am fortunate to have my own cast of characters who have supported me through this series. I'm always thankful to my mother, who encouraged my early love of books and storytelling. To my brothers, who never fail to remind me that one can love ghosts, superheroes, and science all at once.

To Cyril for your patience and support through the long writing days and nights, the joys and the ups and downs. Your dedication to your passion continues to inspire me to never give up on my dream.

To my little boy, I revised most of this book with you sleeping in my arms, which is likely how you learned how to type before you learned to crawl. I'm looking forward to the time when we can read the *Maya* series together.

To my literary agent, Suzie Townsend, thank you for your encouragement and support. You are a tireless advocate, and I am thankful to have you on my team. Thanks to Joanna Volpe, New Leaf Literary Agency's fearless leader and mastermind. To Pouya Shahbazian, the best film agent in the known world. To Veronica Grijalva and Victoria Henderson for shopping *Maya* in the international markets. To Meredith Barnes for your wealth of advice and strategy. To Sophia, who helps to keep me organized. To Kendra, Hilary, Joe, Madhuri, Cassandra, and Kelsey, thank you for your support.

To my amazing editor, Emilia Rhodes at Clarion. I am thankful for your thoughtfulness, sharp eye, and support throughout the *Maya* series. I loved seeing your reactions to Maya's antics. Thank you for giving me a platform to tell a fun adventure story centering Black kids that I never saw when I was growing up.

I am so lucky to have a great team who supports *Maya* at

Clarion. Thank you, Emily Mannon, for heading up marketing and Abby Dommert for publicity. Your work is so key to making sure that people know about the book and getting it into young readers' hands. To Catherine San Juan and the design team who came up with the amazing cover concept for *Maya*. To Elizabeth Agyemang, Erika West, Gretchen Stelter, Emily Andrukaitis, and the whole school and library marketing team at HarperCollins.

Many thanks to the cover artist, Godwin Akpan. Maya and Eleni look fierce. You absolutely nailed it.

To Ronni Davis, you will always amaze me with your energy, kindness, friendship, and humor. Thanks for being with me every step of the way. You are a bright light in my life.

To my ride or die, Alexis Henderson. You read the very first draft of the proposal for *Maya*. Your early encouragement meant so much to me. Thank you for your unrivaled support.

To my Chicago writing family: Ronni (hi again!), Samira, Gloria, Lizzie, Ebony, Zetta, Cathy, Nancy, Irene, Nevien, Anna, Reese, Mia, Lane, and Rosaria. I am in awe of your talent and thankful for your friendship. To the Speculators, who adopted me into their family: David S., Antra, Nikki, Axie, David M., Liz, Erin, Alex, Helen, and Amanda. Thank you for striking up a conversation with a shy writer at her first writing conference all those years ago.

My biggest thanks to the booksellers and librarians for championing the *Maya and the Rising Dark* series. And to the readers (especially the kids) who sent me nice messages. Finally, I owe so much to Mrs. Okeke, whose passion for literature and Shakespeare inspired me endlessly.